It C

takes A

Minute

SASHA LANE

First published in Great Britain in 2022 by Sasha Lane

This paperback edition is the first edition

ISBN 978-0-9934562-4-4

Other titles by Sasha Lane:

Girl, Conflicted

Girl, Unhinged

Girl, Unconventional

Girl, Always and Forever

About the Author:

Sasha Lane is an international selling author of Romantic Comedy novels. Sasha's first hit was with 'Girl, Conflicted' – the first of four books in her 'Girl' series, which has received comparison to the Shopaholic series by the fabulous Sophie Kinsella.

The 'Girl' series follows the main character, Emma Story, as she navigates life in her thirties. The books address serious issues, with humour and fun, helping readers associate with the characters and the real issues that they face.

'It Only Takes A Minute' is the new stand-alone Romantic Comedy Novella by Sasha. This book is the perfect fun read to get you in the mood for your holiday!

Sasha writes books which promote humour, escapism, and the pure enjoyment of reading. Hopefully readers associate with the characters and can see a bit of themselves in them, and they enjoy the journey each character takes.

Sasha works full time in the financial services industry and writes in her spare time, driven by a love of fiction, both romantic comedy and crime due to her degree in Criminology.

SASHA LANE

Chapter One

I stare at the back of the closed front door for what could be five seconds, five minutes, or five hours; I have no idea. It feels like a long time. I would say that a quiet hush has descended on the house in however long it's been since Jacob left, but that would be a lie. The truth is that a quietness has been present for a while now in the house, hanging around like an unwanted scent, trying to make its point. We have been like ships that passed in the night for months, Jacob and I, more like housemates than lovers, and in my heart I knew that the end was coming. I guess we both did.

It still feels sad, though, the end of something that at one time was good, even if the split and Jacob's decision to move out were both very amicable. Four years of my life are now just a part of my past and Jacob will slide into the category of 'someone that I used to know'.

It's strange how someone who once seemed so close is now so distant and will soon become a stranger. I could have argued the point when Jacob said it was over: I *do* still love him, just not in the same way that I once did. But I didn't argue with him. Instead, I offered to move into the spare room (of my own house) so that he could remain in some sort of comfort while he found somewhere else to live. In the meantime, I spent my evenings tossing and turning on the world's most uncomfortable sofa bed without a murmur of complaint.

But that's me all over – amicable, easy-going, never wanting to make a fuss, never doing anything that could even remotely be classed as spontaneous, let alone potentially dangerous or possibly adventurous. I've spent my entire thirty-one years of living on this planet doing the right thing, being sensible, never stepping out of line, doing what was expected of me, and right now, as I sit and stare at the closed front door, contemplating my future alone, being sensible feels like the most stupid decision I've ever made.

'Are you sure that you're completely okay?' Gemma, my best friend throughout my whole life, tips her head to one side and looks at me with what I perceive to be a mixture of concern and maybe a hint of pity.

I roll my eyes. 'For the hundredth time, yes, I'm fine.'

'See, when you say "fine", Kiera, do you actually *mean* fine? Because I've used the word "fine" in the past to mean something else entirely.'

'Gemma.'

'Yes?'

'Shut up and drink your non-alcoholic fizz.'

She sticks her tongue out at me and takes a swig before grimacing. 'Urgh, how much longer until I can have a proper alcoholic drink again?'

'I'm guessing it might be a while. My second godchild doesn't look like it's going to make an appearance anytime soon, thankfully.'

'Ninety-two days and counting.' Gemma smiles and instinctively rubs her growing stomach.

I take a large sip of my red wine: full bodied and, more importantly, with the alcohol still intact.

'It's just that I kind of saw you and Jacob going the distance,' Gemma says. 'You were in love, and compatible, and both enjoyed the same things in life.'

'We did, we were, and I thought we would stand the test of time too, but I guess it just wasn't meant to be. Not everyone gets the full-on romance movie like you and Tom.'

'Full-on romance?' she snorts. 'I don't know about that.'

'Says the woman pregnant with his second child. How did that come about then? An immaculate conception?'

'Point taken.'

I twirl the stem of my wine glass in my hand.

'So, what happens now?' Gemma asks.

I contemplate this question for a minute and then down the rest of my wine before exhaling. 'I continue to live my life…and maybe turn the bathroom into a home spa.'

'And I will create you a fabulous online dating profile.'

I give Gemma a stern stare. 'You will do no such thing.'

Chapter Two

'What do you mean, you're "thinking of going abroad"?' Gemma looks at me with confusion, doing those annoying air quotes, before placing her hands firmly on her hips in her usual overprotective mode.

It has been seven days since the conversation involving the term 'fine'.

'I'm just toying with the idea. You know, sea, sand, cocktails. It sounds kind of nice.'

'You can't possibly go abroad on your own for four whole weeks, Kiera. I mean, what would you do?'

I laugh. 'I don't know. Read books, sunbathe, do some sightseeing. Maybe have an *Eat, Pray, Love* experience.'

Gemma looks unconvinced, a deep frown furrowing her perfectly tamed brows.

I shrug my shoulders. ‘I’d be relaxing. You’re always telling me that I need to take more time out for myself. Isn’t that what a sabbatical is all about?’

‘Not like *this*!’ she huffs.

Years ago, I made a sensible career choice: working in a bank from the day I finished my last exam at school and making my way up the ladder in my practical navy skirt suit and kitten heels. Thanks to my length of service and impeccable attendance record, the bank has given me a four-week sabbatical. It starts in three weeks, and until now I had just intended to do some DIY jobs around the house, maybe repaint my bedroom, perhaps price up actually turning my bathroom into a home spa, and maybe go to a few yoga classes and drink some healthy fruit smoothies. But now, after spending my evenings for the last week watching repeats of God-only-knows-what on Netflix while consuming far too much red wine, I am feeling the urge to just do something unexpected, something very un-Kiera-like, something completely out of the ordinary.

'Are you feeling sad about Jacob leaving? Is this the start of a breakdown? Should I call someone?'

'No, Gemma, I am not having a breakdown, and no, I am not feeling sad about Jacob leaving. Well, maybe I am a little, but I'm fine with the fact that Jacob and I have separated. It had been on the cards for a long time. And if I *was* having a breakdown, then who exactly would you call? *You* are my best friend; that means free therapy sessions with you for life, in case you'd forgotten. Your punishment for being my oldest and dearest friend is that you get to listen to my ramblings without judgement.'

'But on your own? In a foreign country?'

'I said, without judgement.'

'I don't know. It sounds kind of dangerous.'

'Dangerous?'

'You could get mugged, or murdered, or eaten by a wild animal.'

'Eaten by a wild animal?'

Gemma puffs out her cheeks. 'It could happen.'

'I was thinking of somewhere in Europe with a bar and a beach, not the African outback.'

She purses her lips.

'And we live in a city – I could get mugged or murdered on any given Saturday night if I stumbled into the wrong area by mistake.' I drink the last of my coffee and exhale. 'I'm an adult. A thirty-one-year-old woman who is perfectly capable of looking after herself. Is this really about me going somewhere on my own, or is it the fact that you can't come with me?'

Gemma pats her blossoming baby bump. 'I just wish that you'd been more spontaneous *before* I got married and was six months' pregnant.'

'Don't forget my goddaughter too. You already have a child.'

'Believe me, there's no forgetting Marnie. This morning I opened my eyes at the crack of dawn to find her standing at the side of my bed staring right at me with what I thankfully found out, after some severe shock and complete fear, was only chocolate spread smeared across her face.'

I fail to suppress a giggle.

'It's not funny.' Gemma shakes her head. 'Do you know how difficult it is to get chocolate spread out of Ted Baker bedsheets?'

I roll my eyes at her. 'I think the more sensible question here, Gemma, is why, when you have a two-year-old who clambers into bed with you most mornings, do you have Ted Baker bedsheets?'

I leave Gemma's house twenty minutes later and make the short walk back to my home. Gemma is my oldest friend. We've been friends our entire lives and have never lived more than a ten-minute walk from each other. The longevity of our friendship, I believe, is based on the fact that we couldn't be more different. Gemma is loud, confident, spontaneous, and fiercely independent. (Qualities her husband, Leo, both adores about her and is frustrated by in equal measure. Particularly when she demonstrates her loudness on the golf course, where apparently it is a sin to even whisper while someone is on the putting green. And also when she refuses to let him help her carry large items in the garden centre, which has occasionally resulted in his having to pay for a broken item that she's dropped.) I, on the other hand, am quiet, well organised, less spontaneous – a planner, if you will – and I am more than happy to let a man carry a large item to my car for me. What this means is that Gemma and I complement each other perfectly.

Once home, I curl up on the sofa with my laptop and load up a search engine. I type in 'popular European holiday destinations for single people'. A list of suggestions appears on the screen – Barcelona, Madrid, Paris. While they look very exciting and cultural and full of life, they all appear far too busy and hectic for what I have in mind. I'm thinking of somewhere much more peaceful, like a quiet beach with a local bar to grab a glass of wine in and a sun lounger to loll on while watching the world go by. I appreciate that doesn't necessarily sound like the most unexpected and outrageous or out-of-the-ordinary thing to do, but in my world, it's a huge step.

Crete – hmm, it has potential. Feta cheese, ouzo…erm, okay, my knowledge of anything Greek is seriously poor.

Vilamoura in the Algarve? That has a nice sound to it. I click into the link. I've never been to Portugal. The girls' holidays that I went on with Gemma in our younger days were usually to Ibiza or Cyprus – and there was that one ill-fated trip to Magaluf. I shudder and try to bury the memory of the nights of crazy-coloured alcoholic shots, followed by more alcohol, and then some more alcohol, just for good measure. It's a wonder that either of us has any recollection of those seven drunken days, and that we survived for that matter. In all honestly, it's much better if we try to permanently forget.

I scroll through the pictures of the Portuguese coastline. It's stunning. Orange clifftops frame the golden sandy beach and unbelievably blue sea. This is looking more and more perfect by the minute.

Beaches, tick; historic towns, tick – and ooh, what's this? I click on an article with a picture of a delicious-looking pastry. Mmm, anywhere that's famous for a custard tart is definitely somewhere I want to go. I am very partial to a pastry with a nice cup of coffee and the *pastel de nata* sounds like a good-enough reason to pick Portugal over anywhere else. Obviously, I won't divulge to Gemma that I've decided on my destination based on my desire to consume desserts; this will only fuel her 'Are you having a breakdown?' theory.

Now to find some accommodation. I type in the dates of my sabbatical and press the enter key on my laptop. A list of apartments and villas loads up and I scroll through them until I see one that catches my eye. A third-floor, one-bedroom apartment within a short drive of the marina. I click on the customer reviews: 4.5 out of 5. Clean, tidy, and a great location. Sounds good to me.

Before I can change my mind, or even apply some usual Kiera cautionary logic, I select the apartment and enter my credit card details. As the screen updates to confirm my successful reservation I can feel my heartbeat quickening in my chest as it thuds against my ribcage. I inhale deeply, then exhale slowly. Right then, now for the flights.

That night I lie in bed staring up at the ceiling, a nauseating fear washing over me. What was I thinking? Just packing a bag (okay, maybe two) and jumping on a plane to a country I have never been to. Alone. ALONE. What was I thinking? Gemma was right. This is a stupid idea. I'll be murdered the minute I step off the plane. What have I done? What have I actually gone and done?

'So, that's it, you're definitely going?'

I nod, screwing my hands into fists to hide the way they're shaking slightly, the palms sweating, at the mention of my impromptu getaway.

'Definitely,' I say, portraying a whole lot more confidence than I feel, glancing between Gemma and her husband, Tom. It's the following night and we're eating Chinese food together.

Tom, always the voice of reason, takes a sip of his beer, then says in the most calm and rational manner, 'It sounds perfect to me, Kiera. I've never been to Portugal, but from what you've described, Gem and I definitely should.'

'Thank you, Tom.' I press my lips together and look back to Gemma, who remains silent, clearly chewing a mouthful of crispy wonton for far longer than necessary.

Tom intervenes, filling the silence. 'Gemma is excited for you, she is; she just worries about you.'

'I do,' Gemma agrees quickly, before putting a vegetable spring roll into her mouth in what I presume is an attempt to prevent her from saying what she's really thinking.

'And Gemma loves you and she cares about you,' Tom goes on.

Gemma nods along emphatically, still chewing the spring roll as I watch this charade.

'But sometimes she forgets that you're an adult, Kiera, and a very sensible one at that.'

Hmm. I feel like I want to protest at Tom's 'very sensible' argument; however, he's absolutely correct. I am very sensible.

Gemma swallows noisily and rolls her eyes at Tom. 'Just promise me that you won't go wandering off in the dark somewhere on your own,' she says to me.

'I promise.' I pick at the remains of the crispy seaweed.

'Or, worse still, go off with some strange man.'

Chance would be a fine thing.

'I promise not to go off with a strange man, and I won't be walking off anywhere in the dark anyway. I've hired a car.'

This seems to flummox Gemma even more. 'You've hired a car?!'

'Yes,' I say slowly. 'That's what people do. It helps you to get around and see things. Plus, if I'm in a car, rather than on public transport, then I'm less likely to come into contact with any strange men to go off with, or any of the potential murderers that you seem to be concerned about me bumping into.'

Tom tries hard not to smile at this.

'But it's dangerous driving abroad,' Gemma protests.

I wave my hand at her. ‘I drive here all the time; it’s the same.’

‘It is *not* the same. You’ll be driving in the passenger seat on the wrong side of the road.’

Well, when you put it like that…maybe the hire car was a bad idea. I frown.

‘Okay,’ Gemma concedes, perhaps in response to my hesitation. ‘If you’re happy, then I’m happy for you.’

‘I am.’

‘And if you’re adamant that you’re doing this –’

‘I am.’

‘Then I’m excited for you.’

'Great.' I give her my most winning smile. 'Does that mean that I can count on you to drive me to the airport?'

'Of course we'll be there to see you off, won't we, Tom?' Gemma absentmindedly whacks Tom on the arm.

'Of course,' Tom agrees. 'Right, now that that's sorted, who fancies dessert?'

Chapter Three

My last day of work before my impending trip soon comes around and I half walk, half skip up to the bank and swipe my keycard at the door. The second that I step inside the building my enthusiasm deflates like a burst balloon as I bump, literally, into Josie, the twenty-two-year-old wannabe model who turns up every day wearing more makeup than a whole cosmetic counter, and who appears to have no concerns about voicing loudly, and on a regular basis, the fact that she's only working at the bank until something better comes along, either a modelling contract or a sugar daddy; my money is on the sugar daddy.

'So, isn't it your singles' holiday or something next week?' Josie asks with amusement as she leans on the lockers in the staff area, her head lolling to one side, potentially due to the weight of the huge fake eyelashes that she appears to have applied this morning.

I force myself to count slowly to five in my head before responding; otherwise, my response would be to throw something at her. 'It's a sabbatical,' I say, 'and it's not a singles' holiday; I'm just going alone.'

'Whatever.' She flicks her long blond hair over her shoulder, which she does on a regular basis – I assume because she thinks it makes her look sexy. 'Still sounds pretty sad to me.' She shrugs.

'Yes, well, anyway.' My lack of comeback is astounding.

'So, what are you going to do, like, on your own?' Josie crosses her arms and inspects her bright-pink nails.

There are a million things that I could say in reply to that question, and many more appropriate than the one I go with, but for some reason my usual polite inner self abandons her morals and I simply say, 'I'm going to enjoy some sun, sea, and sex.'

Then I brush past Josie, my head held high, inwardly pleased with the look of surprise on her face, outwardly blushing crimson all the way to my desk.

The day passes quickly and without further incident, and it isn't long until I find myself on the drive home, crawling along in the rush-hour traffic. Usually, I would be cursing the string of red brake lights ahead of me, but today I have a smile on my face that no traffic jam can dislodge. Work is done now, and I leave for the airport in…I glance at my watch. Ten hours. The only thing left to do is to pack my suitcase.

As I stand in my bedroom later that evening, the still-empty suitcase perched on the bed, I realise the idiocy of my complacency. When I thought 'the only thing left to do is to pack my suitcase', I almost forgot what a huge challenge this is for me. I struggle with the fact that I want to take too many clothes so that I'm prepared for any weather and every eventuality, and the fact that the budget airline ticket I've purchased demands that I take no more than twenty kilograms. In principle, this may not sound too bad for a fortnight in Ibiza where you would simply be alternating from a bikini to a sliver of dress for the evening, but a whole month in another country…that's a slightly different problem.

I stare at the majority of my wardrobe, which is strewn across the bed, and decide to be pragmatic. I open the case and throw in three swimsuits, a variety of beach sarongs, several vests and pairs of shorts, and my four favourite summer dresses. A week's worth of clean underwear, two cardigans, and a thin jumper finish off the selection. It's Portugal in May: I expect it to be warm and sunny – that's what all the websites said. Lastly, I pack a pair of flipflops, some flat sandals, and a pair of wedges that are more comfortable than they look.

I decide to buy some toiletries at the airport to give me something to do to pass the time while I'm waiting for my flight, and therefore I just add perfume and makeup to the suitcase before gleefully zipping it up, for once without having to sit on it to close it.

I place my travel documents on top of the case, put my jeans, t-shirt, and sweatshirt to wear to the airport at the bottom of my bed, and that's it, I'm all done. I slide into bed ready for sleep ahead of my long journey tomorrow. I just need my mind to stop swirling with thoughts of people getting murdered in foreign countries while alone (I've googled following Gemma's comments), so that I can get some actual sleep before it's time to get back up. Maybe counting sheep actually works, I ponder. At this moment I'm prepared to try anything.

The alarm shrieks loudly in the darkness and I roll over, reaching my hand from under the warm bedcovers in search of the snooze button. The shrieking stops, thankfully, and I snuggle back under the warmth of the quilt.

Wait! I sit bolt upright in the bed and look at the clock. Five minutes past three. In the morning. I squeeze my eyes shut and open them again to clear the sleep fog. I need to get up, get dressed, and be ready for four a.m., when Gemma and Tom will be picking me up to take me to the airport. Today I'm getting on an aeroplane and flying to Portugal. Today is the start of my long-awaited sabbatical. Today there's no time for snoozing – I need to get moving.

After a quick shower, I make myself a coffee and add a spoonful of sugar, which is unusual for me, but it's far too early to try to force some food down and I need the energy kick. I'm not used to getting up in the middle of the night, and my body and mind make no attempt to hide their displeasure at the fact.

I gulp down the coffee while applying the minimum amount of makeup to make me look like a human being, and by the time I'm done I at least look more awake even if I don't feel it. A slight uneasy notion settles in the bottom of my stomach. It could just be from the coffee at three thirty a.m. on an empty stomach, but I suspect it's more to do with the fact that I'm doing something completely out of character. I've never even flown on my own, let alone spent any time alone in a strange place.

I look back at my refection in the bedroom mirror. 'Come on, Kiera,' I say sternly, 'you can do this. You're a grown woman. Stop being a baby. You made the decision to make a change, to do something that you ordinarily wouldn't, and living in another country for a short time is going to be an experience. It's a chance for you to do whatever you want, and *be* whoever you want, for one month. It's just four weeks, so go and goddamn well enjoy it.'

I hear a soft knock on the front door. Well, I guess it's now or never, and really it has to be now. Backing out of this is not an option at this point. So I stand up, pull on my sweatshirt, and grab my suitcase. Portugal, here I come.

I open the door and whisper 'Morning' to Tom as a gust of cold wind whips past me, nearly taking my breath away. I shudder. I hope it's at least ten degrees warmer where I'm heading.

'Gem is in the car. Pass me your case.'

I look at Tom, worried. 'Where's my goddaughter?'

He laughs. 'Don't panic – we didn't leave our two-year-old daughter home alone.'

'I didn't…I mean, I *wouldn't* suggest that you would.'

'Marnie stayed at my mum's last night, so she's perfectly fine. Believe me, you didn't want to see Marnie if we'd woken her at three thirty a.m. to bring her with us.'

'Yeah, it's too early for an angry toddler.'

'Angry? Try a cross between Godzilla and Bigfoot being poked with a huge stick.'

I laugh and heft my suitcase over the doorstep. Unfortunately, I suspect the case may weigh far closer to my allotted twenty kilograms than I had intended, but hopefully not a kilogram more. I lock the front door behind me and follow Tom to the car. He puts my case in the boot as I climb into the back seat behind Gemma.

'It's bloody freezing,' Gemma complains as she turns awkwardly around in her seat, careful not to squash her baby bump. 'I'm only doing this because I love you. There's nobody else that I'd get out of a warm bed for at half three in the bloody morning.'

'I know. I love you too.'

Tom climbs into the driver's seat and we set off for the airport, thankfully with the heating on full blast.

'I'm really going to miss you,' Gemma says as we make our way through the dark and deserted streets to the ring road.

'I'm going to miss you too, but I promise to call every day.'

'Even if you're too busy sunbathing and drinking cocktails?'

I already know the response required for this question. 'I'll never be too busy to call my best friend.'

Gemma smiles widely. 'And you'll video-call?'

Urgh, there's nothing worse, in my opinion. I hate video calls. It's much better when you don't have to remember if you've brushed your hair or applied makeup or got dressed before you speak to someone.

'Of course I'll video-call,' I say – a small white lie. Okay, maybe a big lie, as I have no intention of appearing on a video call.

'And you'll take lots of pictures so we can see what you're up to.'

'You mean, see what we're missing while we're up to our eyes in Play-Doh and glitter?'

Gemma purses her lips at Tom. 'You wouldn't swap.'

He places his hand over her bump and says very sweetly, 'I would never want to swap.'

I smile. They're so cute together. Gemma hit the jackpot when she met Tom. She was slightly tipsy and flinging herself around the dance floor in a nightclub ten years ago when another excited reveller accidentally knocked into her and sent her crashing towards the floor – until Tom swooped in at the last second and saved her from faceplanting onto the sticky tiles, and probably receiving a serious injury too. A true gentleman, and her soulmate. They've been inseparable ever since.

'Are you excited then, Kiera?' Tom asks as I see a sign for the airport. 'In a few hours you'll be gazing out at golden sands while swigging a glass of sangria.'

That sounds so classy. Then again…

I swallow down the flapping butterflies in my stomach. ‘I’m looking forward to some warm sun. It’s flipping freezing here.’

We pull into the airport drop-off, which I’m surprised is so busy for four thirty on a Saturday morning, and Tom stops the car behind a gang of guys piling out of a minibus, already singing and drinking what looks like cans of lager as they stumble out of the vehicle and attempt to allocate luggage to each individual. They’re all dressed in a variety of coloured t-shirts with nicknames emblazoned across the front, clearly heading to a stag do.

Tom jumps out of the car and goes around to the boot to unload my case. I climb out and instantly open the front passenger door to help Gemma out of the car too. As soon as she's made it to an upright position, which takes a few moments, she pulls me into a hug, squashing me against her expanding bump.

'Remember to call every day,' she says into my hair, still squeezing me tightly.

'It's only four weeks, Gemma. I'll be back before you know it.'

She releases her grasp and pulls away, looking sad. 'I know you will.'

'Just look after my new goddaughter until I get back.'

'It could be a godson.'

I shake my head. 'It's definitely another girl.'

'I hope not,' Tom sighs as he wheels my case around to us. 'I'll be completely outnumbered then. Marnie's already starting to show that she's inherited her mother's attitude.'

'Oi,' Gemma protests.

'Terrible twos?' I ask.

Gemma rolls her eyes. 'Let's just hope that it's only the twos, and not the threes, fours, and fives as well.'

I shiver in the morning chill and pull my hands inside the cuffs of my sweatshirt.

'Come on, you two, say goodbye, and then Kiera can get inside. It's cold, and you're pregnant – you shouldn't be standing out here in this weather.'

'I'm pregnant, not ill.'

'Tom's right, Gemma, I don't want you catching your death out here.'

We hug it out one more time and then I take hold of my suitcase and wave goodbye as Tom and Gemma get back into the car. I walk towards the revolving doors that lead to the departure terminal and turn and wave one last time as their car pulls away.

Once inside the terminal I head to the check-in desk. The hot air blowing down from the ceiling starts to defrost my hands as I wheel my case to the back of the queue. Once checked in, and with my suitcase offloaded, I find myself in the duty-free shopping. Along with the necessary toiletries I also manage to purchase two lipsticks, a bottle of perfume, and a Starbucks latte before I finally board the aeroplane.

The window seat is my favourite, as I love to watch the view during take-off and landing; it's mesmerising. Thankfully, there's no-one in the seat immediately next to me, and the middle-aged guy in the aisle seat seems oblivious to my presence, as despite the fact that we're still parked on the tarmac, he's already engrossed in what looks like a huge war novel.

We hurtle down the runway and are soon surrounded by big white fluffy clouds. I must have been crazy to think that this was a good idea, just upping and leaving to fly alone to a different country. It sounds idyllic, but the reality could be anything but. *Well, Kiera, you've made your bed,* as my mum used to repeatedly say to me when I was growing up, *now you can lie in it.*

The stag party from the drop-off point appear to have boarded this plane too, as I can hear their singing from the rear of the plane. I just hope that they aren't staying anywhere near me once we land. I push my earphones in and press play on the music app on my phone (in flight mode, of course), and hope that the relaxing sounds of Adele can calm my nerves and give me some perspective on things.

As the cabin crew make their way down the aisle with the drinks trolley, I am very tempted to order a double measure of gin. But then I remember that when we land I need to be in a fit state to drive the hire car to the apartment from the airport – in the passenger seat and on the wrong side of the road, as

Gemma so kindly pointed out – so it's probably not a good idea to drink alcohol before driving, or on an empty stomach on top of a Starbucks latte for that matter. Instead, I opt for a cup of tea and a bacon sandwich as I count down the minutes until we arrive at Faro Airport, where I will begin my temporary life as my alter ego in the Algarve.

Chapter Four

The flight goes by more quickly than I expected it to and it's not long before we start our descent to land. As the plane slows and we fly below the clouds I stare out of the window at the scene below us. We are flying over what looks like marshland below, and small fishing villages. It looks idyllic. Sparkling blue water glistens in the bright sunlight, and for the first time since I clicked on the 'Book now' button on my laptop, I'm starting to think that I've made a good decision after all, a really good decision. It looks so peaceful and picturesque, and the reality of spending time in this destination suddenly looks incredibly appealing. No work, no annoying Josie, no early-morning commute into the city centre. Just sun, sand, sea, and hopefully cocktails, many, many cocktails.

I'm not at all prepared for the wall of heat that sandbags me the second I leave the coolness of the air-conditioned arrivals terminal, or the blinding sunlight. I fumble in my handbag for my sunglasses before my corneas implode. I'm already sweating, and I've not even made it across the walkway to the hire car office yet. Thankfully, I paid a little extra for a speedy 'click and go' service with the hire car company, which should mean that I type my booking reference into the vending-type machine in the office foyer, retrieve my car keys, and then climb into whatever vehicle I've been allocated so that I can turn on the air-conditioning as soon as humanly possible, preferably before my clothes completely stick to my body like food wrap.

The process is quick, and I'm relieved that it's only a couple of minutes before I'm pulling my suitcase across the tarmacked car park, wiping my sweaty brow and top lip, in search of the Renault Clio which will be my mode of transport for the next few weeks. I spot it at the end of the row and quicken my pace as the late-morning sun burns down on me. Job one when I have unpacked is to buy a large sunhat.

After flinging my case none too gently into the boot of the car, I climb into the driver's seat. Feeling very oddly positioned on the left-hand side of the car, I start the engine and quickly turn the air-conditioning up to full blast. Initially, I am met with a gust of hot air, which is extremely unpleasant, but as I fan my face with my hand, I start to feel the coolness coming through the air vents. As much as I want the sun, I'm regretting my travel outfit choice of t-shirt and sweatshirt with jeans, which I put on far too many hours ago in the chilly UK. I should have braved it and worn shorts and a vest for the flight.

I made sure that the car I hired had satnav as standard. Thankfully, it's already preset to English, so I type in the address of the apartment, look in all of the mirrors, and then tentatively press on the accelerator pedal. Right, stay calm. In the passenger seat. On the wrong side of the road. Bloody Gemma!

I pull nervously out of the hire company car park and onto the road that leads out of the airport, then onto the main dual carriageway. My palms are starting to feel sweaty and not from the heat anymore, and my heart is racing.

'Drive on the right, drive on the right,' I repeat like a mantra as I join the queue of traffic at the roundabout, and then there's no more time to think about things as I accelerate and the little Clio jumps into action and I grit my teeth as I file into the stream of traffic and head away from the airport towards the main town of Faro.

Faro is more hectic than I expected. The road is busy with cars and vans. Huge billboards advertising clothes stores line the road and I pass a shopping centre on my right-hand side, making a mental note to return to that at some point during my stay. I read that Portugal has a good selection of shoes and handbags to purchase, and I intend to make that one of my priorities.

It's not long before I leave the hustle and bustle of traffic behind as I follow the instructions from the satnav and make my way along the ring road, where it is much quieter now. I don't know what Gemma was so worried about, driving here is quite –

'Argh!'

I speak too soon as a small delivery van with pictures of Coca-Cola on the side pulls out from a slip road on the right and nearly runs straight into me.

'Bloody foreign drivers!' I almost shout before the irony of my comment dawns on me. I am the foreign driver here.

I pass restaurants at the side of the road, numerous pottery and garden retailers (one even has a huge watering can prominently sitting right outside it), and, oddly, a large number of vending carts selling massive bags of oranges. How many oranges do people here eat? Although I do like the idea of freshly squeezed orange juice for breakfast. Maybe I should get a bag. I pull over at the next cart and climb out of the car and into the heat again.

'Ola,' I say as the lady manning the cart smiles at me. This is possibly the only word of Portuguese that I know. 'How much?' I point to a huge sack of fruit.

'Five euros.'

'Five euros?'

She nods.

I open my purse and hand over the money, then collect a sack of oranges, and this is where the fun begins. There's really very little space in the boot of the car, given my suitcase, so instead I strap the oranges into the passenger seat, much to the amusement of the vendor. Then, after carefully checking each viewpoint from the car three times, I pull back out onto the road to resume my journey.

Interspersed between the orange vendors are roadside bars and coffee shops. In my limited research prior to this trip, I did read that Portuguese coffee is supposed to be pretty good, although I prefer my caffeine fix in a cup larger than an espresso shot, which is apparently the coffee of choice over here. Maybe life out here is much less stressful so you don't need a gallon of coffee to make it through each day. I would be asleep at my desk by eleven thirty a.m. without my morning fix of two large mugfuls.

It doesn't feel like I've been driving for that long before I'm instructed by the satnav to take the third exit at the next roundabout. The apartment can't be far away, and as I take in the sights around me, I can feel a smile spreading across my face. I turn off the main road onto what can only be described as a dry mud track, and the car bumps along the dusty road. We may complain about potholes in the UK, but really, we have nothing on this. I follow the road, which has now narrowed to less than the appropriate width for two cars, and I hold my breath as I approach a turning under a bridge; it looks like I'm entering a crevice between two rocks. I don't breathe again until I'm out on the other side and the road widens. Thanks, satnav. Couldn't you have picked a more tourist-friendly route? Although I want to experience living in another country, I would prefer not to die while doing it, and I could do without losing a wing mirror before I even make it to my destination. I silently praise my choice to pay extra for the no-excess policy on my car hire. If this road is an example of what's to come during this holiday, the car hire company will be lucky if the car makes it back in one piece.

Five minutes later I take a left turn into a road which leads past some apartments and villas, restaurants, a row of shops and coffee shops, and people wandering around in shorts and flipflops. I long for my own shorts and flipflops, and a shower maybe.

'You have reached your destination,' the satnav announces as I pull into a driveway leading to a number of tall, beautiful apartment blocks, all white and clean-looking, with gorgeous pink flowers climbing up the sides of the buildings. I drive slowly, looking for block D, and pull into one of the car parking bays.

I've finally made it. I'm here, at the beginning of my new adventure. I can't wait to feel the grainy sand between my toes and the surf lapping at my feet. It feels like a very long time since I left Tom and Gemma at the airport departure drop-off this morning, but it has been worth the journey, and now it's time to acquaint myself with my home for the next four weeks.

'Argh!'

A loud rap on the driver's window snaps me back into the moment and for a split second I fear that I'm about to be mugged or murdered or something (Gemma's voice rings loudly in my head) before I've even had the chance to get out of my hire car, and less than an hour since I first set foot in Portugal. But instead, I see a smiling face surrounded by dark curls, and a hand holding up a key. I open the window a fraction.

'I'm so sorry to make you scared, miss,' the man says as he steps back from the car. 'Are you Kiera?'

I nod. 'Yes, that's me.'

'I'm Joao. I am here to greet you for the apartment.' He gestures towards the building.

'Ah. Right, of course.' My heartrate starts to drop back down to normal. 'Hello, Joao.' I close the window and climb out of the air-conditioned car and into another wall of heat. 'Nice to meet you.' I hold out my hand.

‘Can I help you with your bags?’ Joao asks as he shakes my hand. He’s tanned, and has soft, dark eyes which immediately make me feel at ease. Why he’s dressed in jeans and a t-shirt in this heat, I have no idea, but then I glance down and see his flipflops and I smile.

‘That would be great, thank you.’

I walk around to the rear of the car and open the boot. Joao leans in and lifts out my suitcase with ease, and he strides towards the entrance to the building. I grab my handbag from the passenger seat, unclip the giant bag of oranges and scurry after him, trying not to drop the mesh sack, which is heavier than I remembered. Once inside we get into a small lift which looks like it will take three people at a maximum.

'The apartment is on the third floor,' Joao says as he presses the number three button on the lift and it shoots into action. I note he gives the oranges that I'm still grappling with a sideways glance and his mouth twitches at the corners. I'm guessing that I'm not the first tourist he's encountered who's turned up with a suitcase and a large bag of fruit.

Once the lift stops, the doors open to reveal just two apartments on this floor. Joao opens the large white door to Apartment G and wheels in my suitcase. I follow him into the open-plan lounge, which has two comfy-looking sofas and a small dining table.

'The kitchen is just here.' Joao points to a small, tiled kitchen through a door on the left. 'And the bedroom and bathroom are just to the right.' He points. ‘Clean towels are in the bathroom. Sheets and towels are changed on Saturdays.’

‘Right.’ I nod.

‘The shared pool is to the left of the apartment block. There are sunloungers, but you need to take your own towel. There’s also a poolside bar. It serves beer and snacks.’

‘That’s great. Everything looks great. Thank you.’

‘Do you have questions before I leave?’ he asks.

I shrug. ‘None that I can think of.’

He hands me the keys. ‘Then you have my mobile number on the keyring. If you have any problems at all during your holiday, then please call me and I will be happy to help. Enjoy your stay, Miss Kiera.'

'Thank you, Joao,' I say as he steps back out of the apartment and I close the door behind him.

I take in a deep breath and slowly exhale, feeling a huge grin spreading across my face. Right, first things first. Where the hell is the air-conditioning switch? Maybe that should have been a question that I asked before Joao left.

I wander around until I see the switch and I hit the 'High' button and it clicks into life. I wheel my case into the bedroom and abandon it there for a moment as I take a look around. The bathroom is tiled from floor to ceiling like a spa, and fresh towels are piled on the shelf above the bath.

I walk back through the living room, unlock the patio doors and slide them open to reveal a stunning view over the immaculate grounds surrounding the apartments. This place must have a full-time gardener or two to keep it looking like this. It looks like every plant and blade of grass has been hand-snipped to perfection. I step out onto the small balcony, which has two chairs and a table, plus a brick barbeque built into the wall. The smell is intoxicating, a mixture of fresh trees and smoking wood in the distance, mixed with the floral scent from the pink flowers climbing the walls of the apartment block. It smells like heaven. I cannot quite believe that this is where I'll be staying. It's perfect. Stunning, peaceful, and, most importantly, just a short walk from the beach.

I quickly unpack my clothes (i.e. I chuck them, still folded, from the suitcase onto the shelves in the wardrobe) and transfer my toiletries to the bathroom shelf, before peeling off my jeans and t-shirt to take a much-needed cool shower.

Refreshed from the shower, I lather on factor-fifty sunscreen, before pulling on a sundress and slipping my feet into my new flipflops. Throwing my handbag over my shoulder, I put on sunglasses and head back out into the glorious sunshine in search of the nearby sandy coastline.

Across the road from the apartment there is a courtyard with restaurants, bars, and shops, and as I stroll through, I can smell food cooking and hear the chatter of people sitting and drinking beer from frosted glasses. As I come out of the other side of the courtyard, I see a signpost for the beach pointing up a tree-lined road. The villas and houses that line the road are stunning, each one unique and again immaculately presented. I feel like I'm strolling through a film set, with the early-afternoon sun reflecting off the windows so that the houses seem to glisten.

The road climbs a steady incline and I already feel sticky again as I reach the top. I find myself standing on the edge of a red-clay clifftop, just like the pictures on the internet that I scrolled through not so long ago. I walk a little closer to the edge and look down at the golden sand below and the rippling sea gently lapping the shoreline. You can see for miles up and down the coastline – miles of beach and clifftops to my right, and a large built-up area further down the beach on my left. I breathe in the salty air and instantly feel relaxed. I almost skip down the road towards a steep wooden staircase that leads right down onto the sand.

I make my way down carefully, passing children with buckets and spades, and parents carrying windbreaks and overloaded beach bags, until I reach the beach. Taking off my flipflops, I feel the sand between my toes as I wiggle my feet, and I make my way directly toward the sea. The water is cold but welcoming, and as it laps at my feet, I am instantly taken back to my childhood, when every time we went to the coast, the first thing I would do was put my feet in the sea, come wind, rain, or shine. I can't believe I get do this every single day that I'm here. Gemma would be so jealous if she could see me now. That reminds me: I must text her to let her know that I got here safely.

As I stand here with the sun on my back, still wiggling my toes in the sand, it feels almost magical, like anything is possible. This is my chance to have pure fun – exploring, sunbathing, doing anything that I want, doing nothing if I want. And what I want right now is some food and one of those fabulous-looking frosted beers.

I walk back up the wooden stairs and up the hill from the beach to the clifftop, making a mental note to bring water any time that I'm heading in this direction in the future as walking up the incline in this heat is exhausting. I stroll back down the tree-lined street towards the courtyard and pick the bar on the corner, which is white on the outside and has huge white sofas to match both inside and out. There are a handful of people sitting at tables, all eating and drinking, chatting amiably.

At the bar a dark-haired girl is stacking glasses on the shelf. She turns around to face me and smiles broadly. She's beautiful, startlingly so. Dark, smoky eyes complement her bright-pink lips.

I'm taken aback when she says, ''Ello, 'ow are you?' in what is most definitely *not* a Portuguese accent.

'You're French?' I say, then immediately realise that I must sound incredibly rude, or stupid, or both. 'I'm sorry, I didn't mean for that to sound like an accusation. I just…I guess that I expected you to be Portuguese. Now I feel silly.'

She laughs and waves a hand at me. 'No apology needed.'

Gosh, her accent is so smooth and sexy. I love the French accent. I fell in love with it at an early age when we did a pen pal exchange at school and I got to go to Paris at the age of thirteen. I swooned over every French boy who spoke to me for the full five days that I was there, even though I could only understand a tiny amount of what they were saying, and I always vowed to return to Paris. Maybe I should have gone to Paris.

'What can I get for you?' she asks, leaning on the bar, still smiling widely, which looks like her natural expression. I'm a frowner, mainly because I get to work with people like Josie for a living, and as such I am constantly scowling. Gemma keeps telling me that I will get huge frown lines as I get older. What a lovely thought. I decide to spend the next four weeks smiling instead to try to offset and delay the aging frown lines.

‘A cold beer, please,’ I answer, wafting my hand in front of my face to create a breeze. ‘I’m yet to acclimatise to this heat.’

‘You have just arrived, yes?’

I nod. ‘A couple of hours ago. It was freezing cold when I left England this morning.’

‘It makes no difference.’ She swishes her hand elegantly. ‘You do not get used to it, the heat.’

‘Oh.’

‘I have been here for four years now and still too warm for me.’

‘It’s not warm in France?’ I feel dumb for asking, but still.

‘Not in the mountains. I lived in the Alps, near the skiing.’

'Oh, well, I guess that explains it.'

She places a tall, frosted glass of beer in front of me and I take a grateful sip.

'I am Claudette by the way.'

'Kiera.' I take another sip of beer. 'So, if you lived in the French Alps, then how come you ended up here?'

'Ah.' Claudette smiles softly, her cheeks colouring slightly. 'I follow my heart' – she taps her chest – 'not my head.'

At that moment, a tall, dark, and very handsome man slides up to Claudette and says something to her in what I'm pretty sure *is* Portuguese, and she rolls her eyes at him as he kisses her on the cheek. It instantly makes sense: the communication of love, undeniable in any language. His eyes sparkle as he gazes at her, and Claudette gazes back at him.

‘This is Kiera,’ she says. ‘She just arrive in Portugal today.’

‘Nice to meet you, Kiera. I’m Claudette’s husband, Santiago, Santi for short.’ Mr Tall-Dark-and-Handsome holds out a hand and I shake it gently. ‘Are you on vacation?’

‘Kind of,’ I say. ‘I’m taking some time out. I’m here to relax, sightsee, and shop, I guess.’

‘You are here with a boyfriend? Friends?’ Claudette chimes in.

‘Neither.’ I shake my head. ‘Just me.’

‘Well, you picked the right place to do all of those things.’ Santi drapes his arm around

Claudette's shoulders. 'The beaches here, they are fabulous.'

'I know, I just came from the clifftop. The view is stunning.'

'And Claudette, she can tell you where to shop. She knows how to spend money at the mall.'

Claudette slaps Santi's arm gently. 'It is unfortunately true.' She giggles. 'I am French – I love fashion, especially the shoes. It is my culture; I can do nothing about it.'

'A girl after my own heart. It sounds like I could do with taking some advice from you, Claudette.'

'Any time, I will be happy to help. The stores here in the shopping centres have many choices. You will find plenty to like, I am sure.'

‘Okay, well, first things first. Can you tell me what’s good on the menu here?’

‘The crab salad.’ Claudette nods at me. ‘It is delicious.’

I take a seat at a shaded table outside with my beer and enjoy watching the world go by as I wait for my lunch to be prepared, listening to soft beats as they pump out of the speakers. It’s only two p.m. but I stifle a yawn. The combination of getting up incredibly early, the flight, and now alcohol in the mid-afternoon heat is taking its toll. I might need a power nap after my crab salad before I do anything else today.

It's not long before Claudette walks over to my table with a plate of food. She smiles as she places it down in front of me. 'Enjoy.'

Claudette is right, the crab salad is definitely delicious, and I devour it, realising that the bacon roll I ate on the plane was far too long ago. As Claudette takes my completely empty plate and I pay the bill, I promise to call back in the morning.

'We do lovely breakfast too,' Claudette says. 'And coffee to die for.'

I wave goodbye as I step outside and turn to walk back across the courtyard, but instead I ricochet off something solid in my path, and my Prada sunglasses – newly acquired for my trip and extremely expensive – are ejected from their resting place on the top of my head and thrown into the air, before landing with a sickening scrape on the pavement.

‘I’m so sorry.’ A bronzed god stands before me, ruffling his wavy sun-kissed hair with his hand. He’s dressed in a crisp white shirt, which enhances his tan and physique, tucked into navy shorts, and as I glance down, I see navy flipflops. If I hadn’t physically bumped into him, I would honestly have believed him to be a mirage from the heat.

‘You’re English?’ is the first thing that comes out of my mouth – not necessarily the most appropriate thing.

‘Um.’ He looks towards my sunglasses lying helplessly on the ground. ‘Yes. You seem surprised by that.’ His full, pink lips spread into a smile.

‘Yes, no. It’s just…I…’

'As you're in Portugal, you expected everyone to be Portuguese?' The smile turns into a look of bemusement.

I cringe inwardly. 'I guess so. I don't know. I didn't expect French.' I gesture back towards the bar. 'And English. That's stupid, isn't it?'

'Ah, you've met Claudette and Santi. Great people. Great food.'

I nod. 'Yes, definitely, on both counts.' I stare over at my Pradas. 'I should get my glasses.'

'Let me.' He jogs over and retrieves my sunglasses from the ground. 'It's the least I can do.' He wipes at them with the edge of his shirt and I catch a glimpse of his very suntanned, very toned stomach, and my breath catches in my throat. 'I think they might have survived.' He offers them back to me.

I take a second to inspect them and he's right: miraculously, they appear unscratched. 'They're fine, thank you.'

'Okay.'

'I should be going,' I say.

'Oh, of course.'

I start to walk away.

'I'm Dylan by the way,' he calls as he walks towards Santi and Claudette's bar.

'Right.'

He chuckles. 'This is the part when you say "I'm…"?' He holds out his arms.

'Kiera,' I offer, sliding my Prada glasses on to hide my face, fearing that this interaction is making my cheeks crimson.

'I hope to see you around, Kiera.' He disappears into the bar, and I just stare after him like a lustful teenager.

Was he actually real? Or has the combination of sleep deprivation, extreme heat, and alcohol just made me imagine the hottest man that I've ever seen? Shaking my head, I turn and walk back across the courtyard towards the apartment block, and stop at the small supermarket on the corner to pick up essentials.

Once at the apartment, I open the patio doors to let in some air and sit on the sofa with a bottle of water, my thoughts drifting back to Dylan and his washboard stomach. Oh, come on, Kiera, I reprimand myself, what's the matter with you? Anyone would think you'd never seen a man's stomach before. I have, but it feels like a long time ago. When were Jacob and I last that intimate that it involved nakedness? The fact that I can't remember speaks volumes. Maybe that's what I need, a romantic fling with a handsome stranger. Yeah, right. That's what people in the movies do. Go on holiday. Have sex with a stranger. Fall in love. No, what I need to do is focus on why I'm here, and forget about Mr Washboard Abs. Good plan.

There's a 'welcome pack' on the coffee table and, as a distraction, I flick through it as I rehydrate with my water. My eyes feel heavy as I take note of the suggested places to visit and walking routes promising fantastic views of the coastline.

What's that noise? I struggle to open my eyes, feeling groggy as I push myself up to a seated position. I'm still on the sofa, I realise, and the annoying noise is coming from my handbag. I rub my eyes with balled-up fists, and reach over and pull out my mobile phone. Gemma's number is flashing repeatedly on the screen. Oh no.

I click the 'answer' button. 'Hey, Gemma.'

I swallow. My throat feels thick and dry, and I reach for the water bottle I had earlier. The dregs in it are warm and unrefreshing.

'Don't "hey, Gemma" me. Why haven't you called? Where have you been? Do you know what time it is? Anything could have happened to you.'

'One question at a time, Gemma. I was just going to call you,' I lie as I pull the phone away from my ear, having absolutely no idea what time it is. In my sleepy state, she's lucky that I can remember where I am at the moment. I look at the screen – five fifteen p.m. Oh dear, how long was I asleep for? The curtains framing the patio doors are now billowing in the breeze.

'Nothing's happened to me,' I say, 'I'm perfectly fine.'

'You sound like you just woke up.'

I never could lie to Gemma. 'Okay, you're right. I did just wake up.'

'How come?'

'Because I was tired after travelling, and it's incredibly hot, and I had a large beer in the middle of the afternoon, which isn't my usual lunchtime drink; it's usually a strong coffee to get me through to the end of the working day.'

Gemma laughs down the phone. 'You are such a lightweight when it comes to day drinking.'

'I'm sorry that I'm a rubbish friend, and that I didn't call you the minute I arrived at the apartment.'

'That's okay. I'm sure you were just getting settled in, and you're still alive, that's the main thing. So, what's it like where you're staying?'

'It's beautiful, and picturesque, and like something from a travel brochure.'

I hear a huff down the phone.

'I could lie and say it's plain, and cold, and the beer is watered down. Would that make you feel better?'

'No.' Gemma sighs. 'I want you to be somewhere nice and to have a lovely time. I'm just envious. Have you met anyone yet?'

'A couple who run one of the local bars are lovely. She's French, and stunning. He's handsome. They're really friendly, and very cute together, plus their food is amazing.'

'Well, at least that's something. You're making friends.'

'And I bumped, literally, into the most gorgeous man I've ever seen.'

'Oh my God!' Gemma screeches down the phone, and I instinctively hold it away from my ear.

'Why the hell didn't you open the conversation with that? Tell me more.'

'There's not much to tell,' I say as I stroll through to the kitchen to grab another bottle of water before the conversation deteriorates into Gemma giggling like a schoolgirl.

Chapter Five

After a long, cool shower to wake myself up, I pull on a pale-pink sundress and my comfortable wedges and head out for dinner. It seems sensible to go to the one place that's familiar so far, so I walk across the courtyard to the bar, where I can see Claudette carrying plates of food to customers sitting outside. She waves as I walk over.

'Hello, Kiera. Have you enjoyed your first afternoon?'

'Oh, it's been great. Although I've just had a power nap before coming out tonight.'

'Power nap?'

'A little sleep.'

'Ah, well, you look fabulous. I love your dress.'

I think that Claudette is quickly becoming one of my favourite people.

'Sit down.' She gestures. 'I will get you a menu.'

I take a seat at a table on the decked area and breathe in the warm evening air. Claudette returns with a menu, and I order a glass of locally produced wine – when in Rome; plus, I don't think I've ever tasted Portuguese wine.

Two minutes later, Claudette places a glass of red wine in front of me and I take a sip. I quickly realise that the internet should be telling everyone how great the wine is as well as the coffee, and the custard tart.

When Claudette returns a few minutes later, I order a chicken skewer and rice, and then sip my wine, people-watching. For the first time in a long time, I feel like my shoulders have dropped an inch and I'm remembering what it feels like to relax.

Oh no. I sit up a little straighter. Is that…? It is, yes. Striding super-confidently across the courtyard, dressed in another crisp white shirt, paired with navy chinos this time, is Mr Washboard Abs in all his glory. So much for forgetting about him. I pick up my wine glass and turn slightly to my right. Perhaps if I don't make eye contact it will be –

'Kiera?' And here he is. Right in front of me. 'I thought that was you.'

I put my wine glass down on the table. 'Hi.'

'Are you dining or drinking?'

'Um, dining. I just ordered.'

'Oh, great. I'm starving. You don't mind if I join you, do you?'

'Oh. Um.'

Dylan sits down opposite me, apparently having translated the words 'Oh. Um' to 'Please sit down at my dinner table and intrude on my evening, even though we're complete strangers'.

Claudette comes out of the bar and over to our table. 'Good evening, Dylan. What can I get for you?'

'A beer, please, and whatever Kiera here has ordered to eat.'

She nods and walks back to the bar.

I frown, then remember Gemma and the aging frown lines and my mission to smile for the duration of my Portuguese trip, so I attempt a blank expression. ‘What if you don’t like what I’ve ordered?’

Dylan laughs softly. ‘I eat here all the time. I’ve had everything off the menu ten times over. It’s all good.’ He cocks his head to one side. ‘You’re frowning.’

Damn it.

‘I just…’

‘Sorry, I’m forgetting that we only just met. I live here.’

‘You live here?’

‘Yes. Is that so hard to believe?’

‘No.’ I pick up my wine and take a gulp.

‘And you’re…on holiday?’

'Kind of.'

Santi brings a bottle of beer over to our table and he and Dylan fist-bump before Santi turns to me. 'Hey, Kiera. How are you?'

'Good, thanks.' I smile, and he heads back towards the bar.

'Hmm.' Dylan takes a sip from his bottle.

Okay, now he's starting to annoy me. 'What does "hmm" mean?'

'You're not on holiday, Kiera. People come on holiday with family, friends, a boyfriend.' He takes another glug of beer and looks around. 'And I don't see anyone here with you. *You* are here alone. Am I right?'

I inhale, exhale, then purse my lips. I came here for some peace and quiet, and here I am being interrogated by a rather rude – if also, unfortunately, extremely sexy – man who has invaded my space, invited himself to my dinner table, and is now treating me to the Spanish Inquisition.

'You needn't look so offended.'

'But I am offended,' I state.

'Why? It's just an observation.'

'An observation?'

'Yeah.'

It suddenly dawns on me. 'You don't appear to have anybody with you either.'

'No, I don't.'

'How come?'

‘That’s a long story.’

I raise my eyebrows. ‘I see.’

‘You don’t need to take things so seriously.’

I fold my arms across my chest. ‘I don’t?’

Dylan laughs. ‘No. We’re just having a conversation, getting to know one another. I’m sorry if we’ve got off on the wrong foot. Let me try again.’

I gulp the remaining wine in my glass.

‘And I would like to buy you another glass of whatever that was you were drinking, so we can start again. Deal?’

As much as I want to resist, I have to accept that he’s already sitting across from me and we’ve ordered food, so it would be really rude of me to just get up and leave. Plus, he's annoyingly charming. But I'm not going to be swayed by that. Absolutely not.

'I'm going to take your lack of vocal objection as a yes.' Dylan turns and sees Santi taking drinks to a nearby table and he waves and shouts over, 'Another glass for Kiera, please, Santi, when you have a second.'

Santi nods and goes back into the bar.

'Right, now that's sorted, let's start again,' Dylan says.

'Are you just going to interrogate me all evening and ply me with wine?' I ask.

'No, and no. Why don't we take it in turns?'

I raise my eyebrows sceptically.

'Come on, it'll be fun – like speed dating.'

'Speed dating?'

'You've never been speed dating?'

'It sounds like my version of hell.'

Dylan laughs loudly. 'We have very different versions of hell.'

Claudette interrupts us as she appears at the table with two plates of chicken skewers and a fresh glass of red wine.

'Thank you, Claudette. This looks wonderful, as usual,' Dylan says, taking a slice of tomato from the salad garnish on his plate and popping it into his mouth as he smiles broadly at Claudette. I could swear that she swoons back at him before walking away.

I take the initiative while Dylan is distracted by his food. 'Okay. I'll play along, for a little while, given that you've gatecrashed my dinner.'

Dylan cocks his head to one side and grins as he chews on a second tomato. 'Gatecrashed?'

'Okay, I'll go first.'

'Of course.' He waves a hand at me. 'Ladies first.'

I purse my lips and ponder. 'How long have you lived here?'

'Two years.'

'How come?'

'No, no. It's my turn now. You had your question.'

I roll my eyes and cut into a piece of the grilled, diced chicken. Mmm, Dylan is right: it tastes wonderful.

'How come you're here alone?'

I answer quickly: 'I just fancied some time to myself.'

Dylan chuckles. 'Liar.'

'Why do you think that I'm lying?'

He puts down his fork and interlinks his hands on the table. 'People don't just fly to Portugal to get some alone time. You can do that in a park, or on a drive to the coast in England. You don't need to fly to another country.'

I ignore his statement and continue to my question: 'So what made you come here?'

'A job.'

'What do you do?'

'Nope. My turn.'

My God, he's infuriating.

'Are you in a relationship?' he asks.

I take a sip of wine before answering. 'No, but I'm unavailable.'

'What does that mean?'

'My turn,' I say, much to Dylan's amusement. 'What do you do for a living?'

'I design websites and stuff.'

'Oh, sounds…interesting,' I say but clearly don't mean it. I'm not IT literate and only manage to get by with the computer systems at work because I wrote myself very specific instructions during my induction training and I've befriended the IT support guy, Mitch, and buy him a Starbucks coffee every Friday to keep him onside. I don't care if that's bribery. Needs must.

'It's okay, as far as work goes, but I like the fact that I can work my own hours – there's no clocking in and out at a particular time.'

'I get that. I work in a bank, and they're all about the clocking in and out.' I sigh and dig into the rest of my food.

Dylan grins at me. 'See, we're having a nice conversation now, aren't we?'

'I guess we are,' I concede. 'Does it keep you busy, the website stuff?'

'Yeah, busy enough, but I also get plenty of time to go out on my boat.'

'You have a boat?' I try, and fail miserably, not to sound impressed.

He shrugs. 'Sure. I could take you out on it if you'd like?' He places his knife and fork neatly on his empty plate.

'No, thank you.'

'No, thank you?' Dylan repeats, frowning slightly.

My innate politeness takes over. 'Oh, um, maybe.'

'You don't like boats?'

'It's not that.'

He shrugs his shoulders. 'Then?'

‘I don’t really know you.’

‘Ah, you mean I could sail off with you, murder you, and throw you overboard, with no witnesses?’ I sense a hint of amusement in his voice.

‘Something like that,’ I say.

‘Okay.’ He turns his head. ‘Claudette?’ he shouts towards the bar, and in an instant she appears, smiling broadly at him again; it seems to be her automatic response to Dylan.

‘Yes, Dylan, what can I get for you?’

‘You see Kiera here?’ He gestures towards me.

‘Sure.’ God, her French twang is sexy.

‘Well, I’m going to take her out on my boat the day after tomorrow –’

‘I didn’t agree to that.’

Dylan shakes his head at me and continues, 'So, if you don't see her again after that, then it's because I killed her and threw her overboard.'

I expect Claudette to look shocked, but she just giggles girlishly at Dylan and says, 'You are so funny,' as she swishes her hand at him. 'Can I get you anything else to drink?'

I'm glad that the imminent threat of my murder is so entertaining.

'No, I must be off shortly, but thank you.'

'Kiera?'

'No, I'm good, thanks.'

Claudette picks up our empty plates and heads back inside.

'See?' Dylan turns to me. 'There's no way I'm going to kill you now after that, is there? Claudette won't think twice before sending the police straight to my door if you aren't back here safe and sound.'

I chew my lip. The old, back-in-England Kiera wouldn't entertain the idea of setting off to sea with a handsome stranger, but this is supposed to be me living a different life while I'm here in Portugal, experiencing different things. I've never been on a boat before, other than for what I thought would be a romantic trip down the Thames with Jacob, but he complained about feeling seasick the whole time, even though we weren't technically on the sea.

Dylan cocks his head to one side. 'I'm going to take your silence as a yes.' He pulls his sunglasses down from the top of his head and onto his nose, even though the sun is barely still out and is setting in a fabulous orange sunset. 'Do you have a hire car?'

'Yes.' I nod.

'Great. Then meet me in front of the Sports Bar on the marina at Vilamoura the day after tomorrow at ten a.m. And bring sunscreen.' He swigs the last of his beer and stands up.

I contemplate protesting, but in all honestly, I'm excited about a potential boat trip, and after initially being quite frustrating, Dylan seems like he might be good company. Plus, what else do I have on the agenda?

'Fine,' I concede, 'I'll go on your boat, if only to stop you going on about it.'

He nods at me. 'Until then.'

He places two twenty-euro notes underneath his empty beer bottle and I watch him walk away, a confident swagger in his stride.

'He is very cute.'

I hadn't heard Claudette come up beside me. She sits down next to me, and I shrug.

'I guess he's not bad looking.'

Claudette laughs loudly. 'Your eyes, they are sparkling, Kiera.'

'Don't be silly, they're not.' I instinctively put on my sunglasses.

Claudette sighs. 'That hot young man would not have to ask me twice to get onto his boat with him.'

'Do I need to remind you that you have a husband?' I smile questioningly at her.

'Come on, Kiera, I think that Dylan is smitten with you. You can surely see that, yes?'

'I'm only here for four weeks, Claudette, and I'm not here to have a holiday romance. I've come to enjoy some time by myself in the sun and to experience new things. Plus, I don't want to get attached to someone I'm never going to see again.'

'The heart wants what the heart wants, Kiera, and I think you like Dylan too, maybe a little more than you are prepared to admit.'

'I'm here for four weeks,' I repeat.

'It only takes a minute.' Claudette stands up and collects the empty glasses and the euros from the table and she goes to walk away.

'What only takes a minute?' I call after her, and she turns and smiles brightly.

'To fall in love.'

I'm sure that's just a corny nineties pop song. I mean, people don't actually fall in love the minute they meet each other, do they?

I leave the bar and walk back towards the apartment. On the way I collect some charcoal and bits of food from the small supermarket for a barbeque which I might attempt tomorrow evening. The sun is setting, but it's still hot, so after unloading my shopping back at the apartment, I take a coffee out onto the balcony along with a crime novel I picked up at the airport. After that power nap earlier I'm not tired yet, so I sit down on one of the chairs and open the book.

I only get through the first couple of chapters before my mind wanders back to Claudette's last words – it only takes a minute to fall in love. Is that really true? Do people fall in love at first sight, or is that just something pink and fluffy that romance movies want us to believe so that we keep watching, hoping, believing that one day we'll stroll off into the sunset with a handsome lover, to live happily ever after?

Did I fall in love with Jacob at first sight? Maybe. I don't know. Probably not. In fact, I think it took a couple of dates for me to even start thinking that we could have a serious relationship. I found him attractive, of course, and he was, no *is*, polite and a gentleman, but I always kind of felt that our relationship just simmered along rather than boiled with lust and desire at any point, even in the beginning. I was never sure that there was enough of a spark between us, and maybe there wasn't and that's why it fizzled out. But it was always comfortable, and shouldn't that be what a long-term relationship is? Comfortable in each other's company? Comfortable in each other's lives? Even if there is that ripping clothes off and hot steamy sex in the beginning, it's not sustainable. Every relationship moves past that stage.

Maybe I should have made more effort with the romance. Maybe Jacob should have. It's weird, but now, for the first time since Jacob and I called time on our relationship and he moved out, I feel sad that the relationship didn't last. He was safe, and secure, and we did get along for the most part. Maybe I should have done more to try to keep the passion, more of the ripping-off of clothes, and then perhaps I wouldn't be alone now.

I wonder what it would be like to rip off Dylan's clothes. The image of his tanned, toned midriff that I glimpsed the first time we met keeps forcing its way to the front of my mind, which is both pleasurable and disturbing. It's hard to keep the smile from my face and the blush from my cheeks when he's right there in front of me.

But that isn't love at first sight. That's just lust – pure, natural animal instinct. You see a toned midriff, you want to see it again. I'm not in love with Dylan, I'm not even in lust with him. I'll go out on his boat and enjoy the experience, and I definitely won't envisage ripping his clothes off as we sail across the waves. No. Definitely not.

Right, now that's sorted I open my book, and I continue reading until the sun completely sets and the night air cools. I go back inside and remove my makeup before slipping between the cool bedsheets and falling instantly into a deep sleep.

Chapter Six

I wake to the sound of what I think is a leaf blower. Who on earth is using a leaf blower at – I glance at the bedside clock – eight a.m.? Then I remember the immaculately maintained communal gardens and I sigh. I guess that makes sense.

After spending yesterday sunbathing with my crime novel at the beach, it's now time for my boat trip with Dylan. I climb out of bed and pull on a t-shirt as I pad through to the kitchen to make a coffee. I can already feel the warmth from the sun through the kitchen window, so I pull on a pair of shorts while the kettle is boiling and then take my coffee out onto the balcony. The warm breeze feels like it's softly caressing my face and gently waking me up. I take a sip of my coffee and drink in the view. There are lots of pine trees around the apartment complex and the smell of fresh pine lingers in the air.

I drink my coffee quickly, then shower and change into a blue-and-white-striped sundress with a full skirt. For some reason, this feels like appropriate boat attire. I think I'll go to Vilamoura for breakfast first and then try to find a sunhat before I meet Dylan. In this heat, I'll return to the UK with hair resembling straw, and a burned head. Perhaps I'll need one of those old-fashioned hat pins that my grandmother used to have to stop the hat blowing out to sea in the breeze. Do they even do things like that here?

I laugh to myself. 'This is Europe, Kiera; of course they'll sell hat pins.'

I opt for flat sandals today. I'm not sure that I'm ready to navigate the car in a pair of wedges yet. Outside, the sky is that wonderful bright blue, and the sun is already warm. I start the car and turn on the air-con, thankful to have parked in a shady spot so it's not as much of an inferno as when I first arrived, having not used the car since. I passed signs for Vilamoura marina on my journey from the airport not far from here, so deciding against using the satnav, I press on the accelerator and set off.

Only day three of my Sabbatical and I'm going on a boat. Wait until I tell Gemma. Although I'd better wait until I've actually been on the boat or she'll probably panic about my falling over the side and drowning. That couldn't happen, could it? I mean, Dylan must have life jackets on board. I will most definitely not get on the boat without a life jacket – hot man or not!

It's only a short drive, and apart from a near-miss with an irate taxi driver at a roundabout (his fault, not mine, in my opinion; he was going far too fast and didn't appear to even slow down before whizzing across the roundabout), I pull into the car park at the side of the marina relatively unscathed. It appears that Portugal is full of lovely, friendly, and overly helpful people, until you get them behind the wheel of a car.

The heat today is a little less intense than yesterday's sunbathing, although the warm breeze is keeping me on my toes through fear that I'll have a Marilyn Monroe moment in my sundress and flash my underwear to a bunch of tourists. Thankfully,

I'm wearing big knickers just in case, although in hindsight perhaps shorts and a t-shirt would have been a better outfit to opt for today; I'm pretty sure it's not going to be any less breezy on a boat at sea.

After locking the car, I stroll down some cobbled steps and out into the marina in all its glory. White boats of every size are moored, glistening in the sunlight, the gorgeous blue sea lapping at their sides. The whole atmosphere oozes money and glamour, and I feel like I've stepped into a different world. Restaurants line the walkway, each with decked seating areas. I choose one with blue and white décor and take a seat next to the glass barrier overlooking the water.

A waiter heads over and I order a coffee. I wonder which boat belongs to Dylan. I strain my neck to look up and down the rows of boats, but they all look pretty much the same to me. All white, all seemingly named after a woman.

I smile at a waitress as she passes. ‘Hi, sorry, I’ve just ordered a coffee. Could I get a chocolate croissant to go with that, please?’

She nods. ‘Of course.’

As she walks away I turn and stare out at the incredibly blue sea. This view beats any I’ve had on a weekday morning for the last twelve months. I haven’t even been to the beach for so long. The last holiday Jacob and I took was a weekend camping in Wales. His idea, most definitely not mine. The weather was dry, thankfully, but I hardly slept a wink thinking that a whole variety of insects would crawl all over me the minute I shut my eyes. I was tired and grumpy the whole time, but Jacob loved it. Maybe I should have tried harder to enjoy the things he did.

The waitress returns and places a croissant the size of my head down on the table in front of me, along with a coffee. I thank her before taking a sip. Oh my, that is the best coffee I've ever tasted. Lesson one on my quest for new experiences: buy more Portuguese coffee. I wonder how many bags I can fit in my suitcase to take back with me. Although coffee bags, along with the many shoes and handbags that I intend to buy, may equal me having to purchase an extra suitcase to get them home in, and pay the airline an additional luggage fee. This could turn out to be a very expensive trip!

I sip my fabulous coffee as I people-watch, picking at the pastry, enjoying the sweet combination of butter and chocolate. The marina is busy but relaxed as couples and families stroll by in the mid-morning sunshine.

'They serve the best coffee here, don't they?'

I didn't see him approach, but Dylan slides into the seat across the table from me. Sunglasses on. Crisp white shirt. Looking cool and suntanned, and incredibly sexy. I nearly choke on my croissant and take a gulp of coffee to hide my fluster.

He is not sexy. Dylan is not sexy. You are going to get on his boat, and he is not sexy.

'Hey.' Dylan tips his sunglasses down his nose and his clear blue eyes focus on me.

I clear my throat before saying, 'Hi.' I glance around me. 'How did you know I'd be here in this restaurant? Am I being tracked?' I raise my eyebrows questioningly.

He laughs. 'I was taking a stroll and I saw you. Simple as that. Here you are, sitting out in the open for all to see.'

Hmm. I guess that's plausible.

'I'm assuming that it's okay if I join you. I mean, you are on your way to meet me anyway. I might as well have a coffee with you first.' He looks down at my plate. 'And maybe a croissant.'

I realise that I'm picking at the flakes of buttery pastry and licking my fingers. Dylan is looking at me with a bemused expression, then he suddenly raises his arm as a waitress walks past our table.

'Com licença, posso pedir um croissant, por favor?'

She smiles and nods. *'Claro, senhor.'*

'Obrigada.'

I can't help but giggle.

'What? I can speak Portuguese.' Dylan shrugs. 'I live in Portugal.'

'And I have no idea what you just said to her.' I smirk. 'But she seems to like you.'

'I just asked for a croissant.' Dylan looks right at me. 'And you sound slightly jealous, if I do say so myself.'

'Jealous of what?' I take another drink of coffee, not meeting his eyes, trying to appear aloof. Am I that transparent? And why do I feel jealous that a pretty waitress caught his eye – or did Dylan catch hers?

‘Cassie.’ Dylan leans back in his chair, his arms open, resting on the table.

I shake my head. ‘I’m sorry?’

‘The waitress, she’s called Cassie. I come here all the time. I told you they have great coffee, and she knows me, that’s why she smiled.’ He leans forward. ‘And I’m a good tipper.’

The waitress reappears and places a coffee and croissant down in front of Dylan. He immediately takes a bite.

‘So, where are we going on your boat?’ I say to deflect from the whole pretty waitress situation.

Dylan swallows his mouthful of croissant and takes a sip of coffee. 'I thought we would go down the coastline to Faro.'

'Oh.'

'You want to see sights while you're here, right?'

'Yes.'

'Then I'm going to take you to a place where you get a panoramic view of the city.'

'Where?'

'I hope you don't mind a few stairs.'

I drink the last of my coffee. 'How many is a few? Do I need to order another one of these?' I wave my empty cup in the air.

Dylan looks me up and down purposefully and I blush awkwardly under his scrutiny. 'You look like you'll cope.'

I open my mouth to protest, or say something smart back at him, but Dylan jumps up, downs the last of his own coffee, and slips a twenty-euro note under the cup.

'Come on then. The day isn't getting any younger.' And with that, he walks away from the table, waving to Cassie as he steps off the decked area.

Okay. Right. I guess I'd better follow him. I grab my handbag, throw on my sunglasses, and semi-jog after him.

'So, this is my boat,' Dylan announces as we stop in front of a small white boat. It's so clean that it's glistening in the sunlight, making me thankful of my sunglasses to dim the glare.

Dylan gestures towards it with his hand. 'Hop aboard.'

I glance at the boat, and then back to him. This seems like a good idea in principle, but I fear the minute I put a toe on that boat, my equilibrium will fail me and I'll wobble over like a…well, a drunken sailor, if you don't mind the pun.

'Okay, I can see that this may be your maiden voyage.' Dylan chuckles. 'Allow me.' He strides onto the boat and then turns and holds out his hand.

I have no option but to take it, so I hold out my hand and he grasps it firmly as I step cautiously onto the deck of the boat. As expected, I instantly wobble, and I fall towards Dylan, grabbing his other arm for support. Oh my. I feel his toned arm in my tight grasp.

'Well, it's never had that effect that quickly before.' Dylan looks at me, amusement spread all over his face. 'Not ten seconds on my boat and you're already throwing yourself at me.'

I instantly let go of his arm and steady myself. 'I apologise.' I cough to clear my throat and hide my embarrassment. 'I was just a little unsteady.'

He raises his eyebrows.

'The movement. On the water. But I'm fine now.'

'I see.' Dylan lets go of my other hand and heads towards the front of the boat. He presses a few buttons and the engine roars into life.

‘Okay.’ He turns back around. ‘Before we go anywhere, you need to wear this.’ He reaches down and produces a luminous life jacket.

‘Will I need this?’

He shakes his head. ‘Not in the slightest. But I don’t want your drowning on my conscience if you do accidentally fall into the sea.’

‘You aren’t filling me with confidence here,’ I say, looking ominously at the life jacket.

‘It’s fine. I can drive a boat; I even have a licence and everything. Just put the life jacket on to humour me, please.’

I pull on the life jacket and take a seat on a side bench as Dylan takes control at the front of the boat and we move forward, slowly making our way past the other boats lined up and away from dry land.

We sail out of the marina and out to sea, until the coastline fades into the distance. Dylan cuts the engine and the boat just bobs in the water. He leaves his post at the steering wheel and takes a seat beside me.

‘Fancy a glass of wine?’ He leans forward and pulls a cooler box from under the bench seat and takes out a bottle of white wine and two glasses.

‘I guess I could have one. I do need to drive the car when we get back.’

‘True.’ Dylan nods. ‘But we could always get a taxi.’

I smile. ‘I’m pretty sure that the offence of being in charge of a boat while drunk is just as serious as driving while under the influence.’

'A fair point, Kiera.' Dylan pours wine into a glass until it's half full, then hands it to me. 'A small tipple it is.'

He pours himself a small glass, then raises it. 'To a lovely day.'

I clink my glass against Dylan's. 'Cheers.'

I take a sip of the crisp white wine. Wow, that's good.

'How come you know so much about boats?' I ask, genuinely intrigued. I know absolutely zero about boats and have never had any interest. I mean, I never lived by the sea, so maybe that's why.

'We lived on the Cornish coast when I was a kid. My dad was a keen fisherman – for pleasure, not work. He taught me everything I know about boats and being at sea, and I fell in love with being on the water as much as he did. He used to be messing about with the boat every spare minute he had. It used to drive my mum crazy.'

'He doesn't have a boat anymore?'

He frowns a little. 'No.'

'How come you live here then? The Cornish coast is pretty idyllic too. Are your parents still in Cornwall?'

Dylan stands up and looks out across the horizon and I sense a change in the atmosphere.

I put my glass down and stand up too. 'I'm sorry, I've clearly said something wrong.'

'No.' He shakes his head and turns to face me. 'No, you haven't said anything wrong. It's just…' He pauses a second before continuing. 'My mum and dad were both killed in a car accident. Drugged driver. Five years ago.' He swallows.

I'm shell-shocked. 'God, Dylan, I'm so sorry, I…' Words fail me.

'It's okay. I'm okay.' He shrugs. 'I just don't find myself talking about it much nowadays. Not many people here know about my personal stuff.'

'I can understand that.'

'After it happened I kind of fell apart a bit. I'm an only child so I didn't really have anyone to lean on who could understand exactly how it felt. My aunts and uncles did as much as they could to support me after the funeral, but I spiralled. Lost my job, fell on hard times. So when my parents' estate was settled and the inheritance money came through, I just took off travelling. I wanted to escape, to try to get past it, and in some ways forget at least some of the bad stuff from the previous few months. So I drank my way through Ibiza, through Spain, and into Portugal, and here I am.'

'What made here special?'

'The people. Claudette and Santi found me one night, drunk and face down in my own vomit. They took me home with them, made me shower, and sobered me up. They listened to my sob story and then let me stay for the night. They're good people.'

I smile. That's the first impression I had of Claudette and Santi too.

'Plus, Claudette makes the best bacon sandwich you'll ever eat.'

We sit back down, and I follow Dylan's lead as he picks up his glass of wine.

'But that's enough sad stories for this morning, Kiera. It only takes a minute, though.'

'A minute for what?'

'For your life to change. So make the most of every day.'

'That sounds like good advice – advice that I definitely need to take. I just seem to let life pass me by. I want to do more, need to do more.'

'Someone who came to another country, alone, for a whole month?'

I laugh half-heartedly. 'It might sound brave, but it's not.'

'No? How come?'

'Because I got on a plane not to run to something but to run away from something.'

‘And what was that?’

I sip the wine. ‘From myself.’

Dylan looks at me earnestly. ‘I can help you with escapism, starting now. Drink up, Kiera. We have some fabulous sights to see.’

I finish the wine as Dylan takes the helm of the boat and we sail down the coastline. I lean over the edge, watching people jog along the beach, kids play bat and ball in the surf, and tourists sit leisurely at tables under umbrellas at beachside cafés. They’re all dots in the distance, but I can’t help but wonder who they all are and where they all come from.

We glide into the marina at Faro, having sailed the rest of our journey in the quietness of our own thoughts. Dylan parks the boat – do you park a boat? Anyway, he steps onto the wooden jetty and then turns back to me, holding his arm outstretched. This time, I take his hand gratefully and he guides me back onto solid ground.

We walk across the road and through some cobbled streets until a large, open square appears before us. It's beautiful: lined with old stone buildings, with luscious green trees planted intermittently in between the cobbles.

'And here we are.' Dylan stops in front of a stunning church. I stand and look up to take in its beauty – a white-painted frontage with a bell tower on either end. 'Are you ready?'

He takes my hand and leads me into the grounds of the church. We pay the entrance fee and then wander into the main body of the church. The walls are lined with intricate gold decorative pieces which must be worth a small fortune. I can't believe the detail and the volume of bling in here.

We climb what must be thousands of stairs, along with other tourists, all speaking different languages and pausing to take photographs as they go. When we reach the last cobbled stair, the rooftop opens up, like we're standing on the top of a castle turret, and the entire city is laid out before us in all its glory.

'Oh, wow!' I exclaim, turning around to take in the whole panoramic view. Dylan wasn't wrong; it's the best view I've seen since I got here. 'You must be able to see for miles.' I hold my hand above my eyes and stare out.

'You can see the airport really clearly.' Dylan points. 'A plane is coming in to land right now.'

'How come you know about this place?' I ask him, watching his expression intently. 'You don't look like the church-visiting kind of person.'

Dylan shakes his head. 'I have no idea what that means, but I don't just sit around on my laptop all day. You need to understand the place you're living in, learn its culture, its history.' He frowns at me. 'You're amused, Kiera.'

'No, no, not amused. Maybe just surprised.'

'In a good way, I hope.'

I simply nod and take out my phone. 'I need to take some pictures of these views.'

We make our way slowly back down the steep staircase a couple of minutes later. I follow Dylan, my hand brushing the cool stone wall just in case I take a tumble, which is very possible.

As we step outside, the sun is blinding in contrast to the cool, shaded church, and even with my sunglasses on, I need to blink a couple of times until my eyes adjust.

'Coffee and cake next, I think,' Dylan says. 'This way.'

He walks towards the corner of the square, and we make our way back through the cobbled streets until we reach the bustling centre of Faro. People are on the beach, kids with buckets and spades, and it seems surreal to have a busy town centre right next to a tourist beach. I guess this is a combination of both worlds.

Dylan leads us up a small street lined with shops, and I take in a number of ladies' fashion shops and make a mental note.

Dylan chuckles. 'You can come back here with Claudette. I draw the line at clothes shopping.'

'Would it make you uncomfortable?'

'Show me a man who *is* comfortable hanging around in women's clothes shops, or even worse, outside a changing cubicle.'

'Fair point.' I laugh, remembering a very similar conversation between Gemma and Tom.

I follow Dylan into a coffee shop, thankful to find the air-conditioning on. All this walking around and climbing stairs has made me feel slightly sticky in the midday heat, and that's not a great look.

'What would you like?' Dylan asks as we stand in front of a large display of beautiful-looking cakes.

I look over them all, salivating, and then I spot it. 'One of those,' I say, pointing to the *pastel de nata*, 'and a coffee, please.'

I take a seat while Dylan orders our food and drink in perfect Portuguese. The young barista blushes slightly as he says something else to her that I can't understand but assume is charming. I roll my eyes; this is becoming a common occurrence.

Dylan places the pastry and coffee in front of me as he sits down at the table across from me. A huge piece of chocolate cake sits on his plate, and I smile.

'What's so funny?'

'Nothing.' I shake my head, then take a bite of the *pastel de nata*. 'Mmm.' I touch my lips, licking a rogue flake of pastry from the corner of my mouth. 'The reviews were right; this was so worth the plane ride.'

'What did you just say?'

I swallow, enjoying the taste of the sweet, sweet custard, then say nonchalantly, 'What do you mean?'

'You came all the way to Portugal for a custard tart?' Dylan looks at me incredulously.

I pause, the pastry halfway to my mouth. 'I didn't say that.' I clear my throat. 'I mean, the reviews said…' I close my mouth, feeling stupid, and I lower my eyes to avoid Dylan's gaze.

He bursts out laughing, rocking back in his chair as he reaches for his coffee cup. I drop the rest of my tart indelicately onto the plate, flakes of pastry flying everywhere. My hands fall into my lap.

'Oh, Kiera.' Dylan slurps his coffee before placing his cup back down on the table. 'You are funny.'

Now I'm provoked. He's laughing at me.

'Why? Because I googled Portugal and a bloody pastry was one of its best selling points?' I huff, folding my arms across my chest.

He looks at me, all serious now. ‘No.’ He shakes his head. ‘Because make out that you are “Miss Sensible”, and now I find out that the pull of a custard tart got you all the way to Portugal!’ He grins. ‘That’s the least sensible thing I’ve heard in a long time.’

I want to be mad at him, to defend myself, but in all honesty, I too can see the funny side of this. When you put it like that, it does sound crazy, and a Portuguese tart isn’t the only reason I chose to come to Portugal, but I can’t say that it didn’t influence my decision.

‘I also heard that they have great shoes,’ I retort defiantly, picking the tart back up from my plate. This just serves to make Dylan laugh harder.

'Oh, that's brilliant, Kiera.' He's still chuckling. 'I like that.' He scoops up the last of his chocolate cake and licks the fork emphatically. I wonder how someone with such muscle definition can even eat cake and keep such a good physique – then I shake my head to remove that image. I do not need to be thinking about Dylan's washboard stomach while I'm trying to make a stand.

'See, this is funny,' Dylan says, his laughter subsiding.

'It is? Why?'

'Because I like you.'

I press my lips together.

'And I think you like me too.'

I lick my lips nervously.

'I know you feel it too, the chemistry between us. It's definitely there.' He looks at me confidently. 'This is where you say that you feel it too.' He gestures at me.

I chew my lip now. 'It doesn't matter how' – I cough – 'or what I feel.'

He looks confused. 'And why is that?'

I shrug. 'Because I'm only here for a couple of weeks, and then I go back to my old life. I can't afford to…'

'To have feelings for somebody? How many times have you met someone and had that instant click, that connection?'

I know that Dylan is right. The butterflies in my stomach confirm this. But I can't do this. I can't have feelings for someone and then walk away, and I'm not up for some lame holiday romance.

'I'm only here for a few weeks,' I repeat meekly.

Dylan shrugs. 'So we'd better make the most of it.'

He pulls me to my feet and wraps his arms around me, pulling me in close. His lips brush mine, and I close my eyes, feeling the intensity, matched with the weakness in my knees. This is lust, I say sternly to myself as his firm, toned body presses against mine, just pure lust. But as my body defies me and I find myself kissing him back with wanton desire, right there in the middle of the coffee shop, for once not caring about such a public display of affection, I fear that this is something more than lust, something far, far more.

The rest of the afternoon is a blur as we stroll hand in hand around Faro. I do the usual touristy things, taking photos at every opportunity, collecting souvenirs, until we arrive back at the boat.

As we sail back into the marina, I glance at my watch. It's five p.m. I had completely lost track of time this afternoon and the marina is starting to get busy ahead of the evening trade Dylan helps me from the boat. 'So, do you have any plans this evening?' The words fall from my mouth with ease. 'We could have dinner?'

We stand face to face.

'I would love to have dinner with you, but…'

'But?'

Dylan sighs. ‘I have a client thing.’

‘Oh.’

‘We could meet later, after dinner.’

‘After dinner, as in…?’

Dylan smiles coyly. ‘Meet me at the beach at, say, ten o’clock.’

‘Ten p.m.?’

‘Yes.’

‘You want me to meet you at the beach at ten this evening?’

‘Yes.’

‘Why?’

'God, you're exhausting. Can you just trust me and be there?' he says. 'For now, though' – he glances at his watch – 'I'm sorry, but I need to go.'

'Okay, sure, I'll trust you. I mean, it's not like I only just met you and now you want me to meet you in the dark on the beach.'

Dylan looks at me, amused. 'You came out on my boat, didn't you? And I didn't throw you overboard. I gave you a life jacket.'

'That's fair.'

'So, I'll see you at ten.'

I nod, and Dylan goes to walk away, then he turns back around. 'One more thing.'

And then he steps forward and kisses me passionately, before strolling away leaving me tingling.

In all the times I saw a film with a skinny-dipping scene, I didn't really believe that these things *actually* happened. But here I am, standing on a beach in the dark, watching a far-too-good-looking man take his clothes off, and although my head is telling me not to, I'm starting to peel off my own dress.

'What if people are watching?' I say in a hushed tone, regretting the time I took applying makeup and styling my hair earlier this evening. I'm also regretting the two large glasses of wine that I drank for courage with my dinner. I think they're clouding my judgement.

'Then they have a choice.' Dylan smirks. 'They'll either look once, or twice.'

I stop, mid-undress. 'It's not that simple.'

'You think people will call the police if they see me in my underwear?'

I look him up and down, and he raises his eyebrows at me, causing me to blush wildly. 'Um.'

'What about if I do this?' He removes his underwear, and I have to look away to refrain from staring, gasping, or doing anything else that's wholly inappropriate, or maybe is appropriate, when somebody strips naked in front of you on a public beach.

'Come on, Kiera, don't be shy.' He cocks his head towards the sea. 'I'll be in there waiting for you.'

I stand, unable to move a muscle, as I watch Dylan's very naked bum cheeks jog towards the shore and then descend into the dark-blue water. I'm standing, half undressed, feeling somewhat vulnerable – but, I concede, maybe not as vulnerable as the naked man in the water. Perhaps I should join him. Against my better judgement, I continue to remove my clothes, underwear and all, and, shutting my eyes, I too jog towards the sea.

'Fucking hell!' I exclaim as the freezing-cold salty water laps against my warm skin. I do *not* remember this part in the movies.

'It awakens the senses, doesn't it?' Dylan swims over to me and we both stand, feet on the seabed, crouched so that our bodies are submerged in water up to our necklines.

'Why did I let you talk me into this?'

Dylan laughs. 'You didn't need much convincing.'

'I beg to differ,' I protest.

'You know what helps?' Dylan steps closer to me until we're standing only centimetres apart. My heart hammers in my chest. 'Body heat,' he says, sliding his arms around me.

My senses are heightened from the cold, and the feel of his touch on my wet skin sends a current of electricity surging through my body. As he leans in close and kisses me, I kiss him back with unexpected urgency, and as his fingertips caress my lower back, I nearly lose myself.

'Let's get out of here,' he whispers in my ear and my stomach flips. I know it's crazy, I know it's stupid, I know that I'm only here for a couple of weeks, but oh my God, I want this man right now.

He takes my hand, and we stride from the water. The wind whips around us, and somehow I refrain from swearing loudly again. My teeth chatter as I struggle to pull dry clothes over my soaking-wet skin. We're both giggling as we fight to get dressed.

'Come on,' Dylan laughs, 'before someone actually does see us.'

We make our way across the sand and back up the wooden stairs. It feels like a full-on hike by the time we've made it to the top of the slope and finally around to the villa-lined road. I feel like I'm in a daydream as we walk up the road to the village square. I can hear the music from the cocktail bar on the corner; a live singer who sounds just like Rod Stewart is crooning into the night air.

It's like we're on autopilot. No words have been spoken between us, but we both know that we're heading back to Dylan's apartment, and we both know what that means. We're crossing a line that we can't walk back from. But in the heat of the moment, and having already seen him naked, I don't feel fully in control of my emotions or actions, and whether this looks like a good idea tomorrow in the harsh light of day, right here and now I'm caught up in the passion of the moment. It's exhilarating, and consuming, and to hell with anything else.

Chapter Seven

I open one eye, then the other. It's bright. This isn't my apartment. This isn't my bed – the sheets feel far too soft for starters. This is Dylan's apartment.

I roll over, but the other side of the bed is empty. In fact, the whole apartment is silent. I sit upright and glance at the partially open bedroom door. Visions of last night play like a movie in my head and I close my eyes, pressing my palms into them, trying to squish out the images.

What were you thinking?

You slept with him.

But he is kind of cute.

I shake my head. So not the point, Kiera, so not the point.

What happens now?

I can't think about that; I just need to get out of here.

How could you be so stupid, Kiera? You aren't going to be able to avoid him for the next few weeks.

Why do you want to avoid him?

I cannot form a relationship with Dylan. I cannot fall in love with him. This is just some stupid holiday romance fuelled by very good Portuguese wine and my sorry self-esteem. Right, Kiera. Get up, get dressed, and get the hell out of here before you actually have to face the reality of this situation. If you don't talk about it, then it didn't happen. Good plan.

I pause. That sounds like the most sensible logic and the most insane logic all at once. But who am I to argue? This is unprecedented territory, so I'll take my chances. Now, where the hell are my knickers?

I slide out of bed and scramble around collecting my dress and underwear from the floor, then quickly slip them on as if being fully clothed will erase this situation. I tiptoe through the bedroom door as quietly as I can and step out into the open-plan living area. It's silent. I tiptoe into the kitchen. No sign of him in there either. The apartment is completely empty, no sign of Dylan, and now I feel annoyed rather than guilty for running out of here. Where the hell is he? How dare he leave me here all alone?

Oh my God, was it bad? Was *I* that bad? I don't remember it being bad. In fact, I remember it being very good.

Okay. I think the best thing for me to do is leave and figure out how to deal with this situation later, preferably when I've had a large cup of coffee and have erased last night's images from my memory. I see my sandals near the door and take that as a sign, but just as I grab my handbag from the back of the sofa, I hear the key in the front door lock and my heart lurches.

'Hey.' Dylan steps into the apartment looking incredibly fresh this morning, with only the slight crinkle in his hair giving away the fact that he's just got out of bed. He's carrying a brown paper bag, and after closing the door behind him he holds it up.

'Pastries.' He smiles, then he takes in my appearance and frowns. 'You're going?'

I'm flustered – flustered about sleeping with him last night, flustered about waking up totally naked in his bed, and flustered about his catching me trying to sneak out of his apartment. 'Oh, um, yes, I'm going. I have that, um…I'm meeting Claudette.' I lie.

He nods. 'Right.'

'So, I'd better be going. Bye.' I step around him, open the door, and don't look back.

Out on the street, the sun is already burning and I'm hot in last night's dress as I hurry towards my apartment building, ignoring anyone around me as I fully expect them to be judging me as I do the walk of shame.

What the hell were you thinking, Kiera? This is totally not something you've ever done before. I've had two serious boyfriends, and with both guys I took time to get to know them before jumping into bed. I met Dylan a few days ago, and I'm not supposed to be sleeping with him.

I make it to the apartment quickly and hurry up the stairs; it's too hot even at this time of the morning to bother getting into the sweaty lift. As soon as I've walked into the apartment I switch on the coffee machine and the air-conditioning. It's warm and stuffy, which is not helping my slightly stunned and lack-of-sleep status. Lack of sleep, hmmm.

I close my eyes, reliving the feeling of Dylan's touch on my bare skin. His soft, full lips as they pressed against mine. The slow, sensual lovemaking, then falling asleep in the crook of his arm. And then waking this morning to an empty bed. An empty bed because he went to get breakfast pastries, you idiot. And you just left. Why did you do that? Because you're an idiot? I don't want to answer that.

I grab a mug and press the button for an extra-large coffee and head to the bathroom for a cool shower.

I sip my coffee, feeling refreshed from the shower, if still mortified at my dash from Dylan's apartment. The way I see it, I have two choices. I can ignore the situation – not very grown up, I admit – which will mean avoiding all of the places I've been to since I got here so that I don't see him for the rest of my time here. But it will be near-impossible not to bump into him, and truthfully, I don't want to *not* see him. So that leaves me with choice number two: I have to go and face him and try to explain my behaviour.

I pad out onto the balcony, still in my dressing gown, and sip the rest of my coffee as I stare out over the view. The smell of pine trees is particularly potent this morning and I inhale deeply, closing my eyes. How have I gone from being the most sensible girl to running scared from a man's apartment – a hot man, I might add, a hot man whom I actually really like? I shake my head. Well, Kiera, I guess there's no time like the present.

I brush my teeth, get dressed, and apply makeup, then spritz on perfume before leaving my apartment and retracing my steps to Dylan's.

I stand in front of his apartment building. Now that I'm here I'm wondering if this is the best idea. I scuttled away from him not an hour ago and now I'm back expecting him to give me the time of day. Well, Kiera, you've made your bed.

I press the buzzer for his apartment and wait. Nothing. Is it rude to press it again? Maybe he didn't hear it. I press the buzzer again and wait.

Shit. He's definitely not in. Deflated, and unsure what to do now, I simply stand and stare at the door to the building.

‘Pressing it three times would be bordering on rude.’

My pulse quickens at Dylan’s voice behind me. I slowly turn around to face him.

‘Hi,’ is my grand opening.

‘Hi.’ Dylan cocks his head to one side. ‘Forgive me if I’m wrong, but aren’t you the girl who ran out of my apartment this morning?’

I swallow nervously. Is he angry or making a joke? ‘Yes.’

‘After we spent the night together?’

‘Yes, that was wrong, but –’

‘And I’d brought freshly baked croissants.’

‘I know, yes.’

'Hang on a minute, which bit was wrong?'

I'm confused. 'What?'

'The running out of here, or the spending the night together part?'

I glance around. 'Look, can we talk somewhere a little more private, please?'

'Do you want to go back to the scene of the crime?' Dylan smirks.

I glance up at the apartment block. 'Maybe a walk on the beach?'

Dylan nods, and we walk, awkwardly and in silence, along the road to the square across from my apartment. We continue in silence as we make our way up the road, past the big villas, towards the clifftop.

Dylan speaks first. 'You do realise that at some point you're going to have to talk to me.'

'Yes.'

'I mean, you came over to my apartment. I presume it's because you had something to say, not because you want to…do this.'

'I did. I do.'

'Okay then.'

I look at the ground, glance sideways out of the corner of my sunglasses, and say, 'I'm sorry.'

Surprisingly, Dylan chuckles. 'Sorry for which part? Going skinny-dipping, going back to my apartment?' He leans towards me and whispers, 'Or making love?'

I stop walking – conveniently, as we reach the clifftop. I look tentatively over the edge.

'It can't be that bad.' Dylan peers over the edge of the cliff next to me.

'What can't be?'

'The reason that you left me looking foolish with a bag of pastries this morning.'

'Oh.'

'So?'

'I was embarrassed.' I shrug. 'I don't know why.'

'You do know why; you just don't want to tell me.' He cups my shoulder and turns me to face him. 'What are we doing here?'

'I only just met you. I went on your boat. You kissed me –'

Dylan raises his eyebrows. 'You kissed me back.'

'And we slept together.'

'This is an accurate recap.'

'And I woke up and you were…gone.'

Dylan's eyes widen. 'You ran out on me because you thought I had left?'

'I was…I don't know…I thought…'

'You thought I'd loved you and left you, literally, and that hurt your feelings.'

I suck in my cheeks. 'Did it hurt your feelings when you came back and found me leaving?' I challenge.

He shrugs. ‘I was…intrigued.’

‘Intrigued?’ I try hard not to smile.

‘Well.’

‘Do you have many women running out on you after you sleep with them?’

Dylan shakes his head, chuckling. ‘No. Plus there haven’t been that many women.’

I look right into his eyes. ‘There haven’t?’

‘I don’t know what you take me for, Kiera, but I don’t sleep around. I slept with you because I like you; I already told you that I like you.’

‘The truth is, I don’t know what we’re doing here. I *do* like you, but I’m only here for three and a half more weeks.’

‘And then what?’

‘Then I go back to England, and back to my old life.’

‘So this can just be a three-week thing?’

‘Can it?’

‘What do you say to us enjoying spending some time together, eating, drinking, sightseeing, and just, you know…’

‘Like friends with benefits?’

Dylan cocks his head to one side. ‘I mean, I wasn’t going to phrase it quite like that, but I’m in if you are?’

I consider this for a moment. Can I really spend time with Dylan and not have feelings for him? I already get that excited feeling in the pit of my stomach every time I see him. We slept together, and it was great. But I'm only here for a couple of weeks. I can't fall in love with him, I can't. I'm having so much fun with him, though, and I want to keep seeing him.

I nod. 'Okay.'

'So you'll be my friend with benefits?'

'I'm prepared to give it a go.'

'Good. Now that's decided, let's go for a beer.'

'It's barely eleven a.m.!' I protest.

'Do you have anything else you need to be doing right now?'

'No,' I answer sulkily.

'Then come on, there's this great beach bar I know. I'm away in Porto for the next few days so I won't get to see you as your friend, or anything else for that matter.'

Dylan takes my hand and I stifle a girlish giggle as he leads me down the wooden stairs and onto the beach.

Chapter Eight

After Dylan and I part company at around midday, I spend the afternoon sunbathing by the pool, reading a book, and generally only moving to consume food and drink, then in the evening I loll on the balcony with a glass of wine and a Chinese takeaway.

I spend the next two days strolling along the beach in both directions, taking photographs at every opportunity, and sampling locally produced coffee, and wine, at every beach café along the way.

As I walk along the sand at a leisurely pace I'm passed by numerous people of all ages, shapes, and sizes, jogging along the sand; many barefoot. I couldn't think of anything worse in the Portuguese sunshine. I'm starting to acclimatise to the heat but still lather myself in Factor fifty sun screen before I leave the apartment.

The following morning, I shower and dress in smart white shorts and a navy vest with my wedges, and then wander through to the kitchen and open the fridge. I'm greeted by the huge watermelon that I thought would be a good purchase, healthy and refreshing. I realised my first error when I had to carry the bloody thing back to the apartment. My second error was not appreciating that a watermelon of that size can feed a hungry family of eight. I lug it out of the fridge and hack away at it, nearly losing a finger in the process, then stand slurping on the slices while leaning over the sink, aware that eating very juicy red melon in a pair of white shorts is not the best idea.

Three slices in and I abandon it and instead take a coffee and some toast onto the balcony, taking a seat at the table. My phone buzzes and a text from Gemma flashes on the screen. I click into it while taking a bite of toast, and a photograph of Marnie appears on the screen. By her cute smiling face is the caption, *Morning, Auntie Kiera! Love, Marnie*. I grin at the phone. Gemma got lucky with Marnie. She slept through from the early on, and is bright, confident, and pretty well behaved most of the time. I can't help but think that Gemma should have called it a day with just one. Isn't it fate that her second child will be a Tasmanian devil who can survive on two hours' sleep? I chuckle at the thought and message back:

Hi, Marnie! I miss you. Have a great day at nursery. Sending you love and kisses xx

A car horn beeps below, and as I stand and look over the balcony, I can see Claudette in her car. I shove the last bite of toast in my mouth and take my cup and plate through to the kitchen sink, then grab my handbag on my way as I head out of the apartment and into the lift.

'Good morning.' Claudette smiles as I open the passenger door and climb in.

'I'm so excited for our day of shopping. I've read such good things about Portuguese shoes and handbags.'

'It will not disappoint, I am sure.'

'Excellent.'

I clip in my seatbelt as Claudette finds the accelerator, and we dart forward and then zoom out of the apartment complex onto the main road. This sets the tone for the whole journey, and I cling to my handbag. Claudette talks constantly throughout, a mixture of English, French, and Portuguese, but I wish she would simply focus on the road. I'm very grateful when she swings into a car parking space at the shopping mall and we finally come to a stop.

After three hours of retail therapy, and me probably reaching the point of being one purchase away from receiving a fraud check from my bank due to the spending on my credit card, we decide to take in some sugar and caffeine. As we sit together, I confide in Claudette about my 'friends with benefits' relationship with Dylan.

'We both decided that it's a three-week thing.'

'A three-week thing? I do not know what this means.'

'You know, it's casual, not serious, just having some fun. Friends with benefits.'

'Is that really a thing?'

'Sure,' I say, maybe a little unconvincingly. Claudette looks at me with raised eyebrows. 'We both know that I'm only here for a few weeks and then I go back to the UK.'

'And that's the end of it?'

'It has to be. Dylan lives here. I live in England.'

'And that cannot change, why?'

'Change?'

'Yes.' She nods. 'You live in England now, and Dylan is here. You can live here.'

I laugh. ‘What, are you suggesting that I just pack up my life in England and move to Portugal? Who does that?’

She grins. ‘I did that.’

‘Oh, yes, that’s right, you did.’ I feel bad for making light of her suggestion now. ‘But you hadn’t just met Santi, had you? I mean you can’t just up and leave the life you have and start again somewhere else at the drop of a hat.’

‘Why not?’

Well, I suppose that’s a very good question.

‘I don’t speak Portuguese,’ I say, standing firm on my opinion that this is a stupid idea.

'There are many ex-pats living here in Portugal. There are English-speaking jobs. But Portuguese is not that hard to learn.'

'You speak fluent Portuguese, not just the odd word?'

Claudette chuckles. 'But of course. I live in Portugal. I also speak English, French, and a little of German.'

Of course you do. This is not helping my argument.

'Well, that's all academic, because it doesn't really matter. Like I said, this is a three-week thing.'

Claudette shrugs. 'If you say so, Kiera.'

I take a drink of my iced tea. 'What is that supposed to mean?'

Claudette chews her lip as though she's thinking about what to say. 'It means that I have known Dylan for a while now, and I see him with you.'

'Okay.'

'And it's obvious, to me at least, that he is not just with you for a…how did you put it? Casual thing.'

'But we agreed, no commitment.'

'You can say whatever you want, but the heart' – she jabs her chest with her forefinger – 'the heart wants what it wants.'

Well, this is all very unhelpful and Claudette is not taking my mind off anything here; in fact, she's confusing me more than ever. Maybe this is something that requires Gemma's opinion. Yeah, I kind of already know what she would say, so maybe not.

After a long day of retail therapy, Claudette drops me off at my apartment and we hug goodbye.

'Thank you so much for today; I really enjoyed it,' I say, climbing out of the car.

'It was fun, yes.'

'Yes, definitely. We must do it again before I leave, but maybe just window shopping.' I laugh. 'I'm not sure that my credit card can take another hit.'

Up in my apartment, I shower and change into one of my new purchases, a long navy-and-white-striped bodycon dress, which sticks to me like cling-film despite my shower, and go out onto the balcony. The evening sun glares hot and orange on the horizon. I light the barbeque on the third attempt – honestly, I never understand how anything spontaneously sets on fire. I can remember spending an hour trying to light the log fire when Jacob and I went to a cottage in the forest for the weekend.

I pour a large glass of chilled Portuguese Sauvignon Blanc, which is almost as nice as the New Zealand one, as I prepare a steak and a chicken kebab, and make a fresh salad. As the meat sizzles on the barbeque, I nibble on some feta cheese and olives while I sit on the balcony and look out at the view of pine trees and other apartments in the distance. This truly is a beautiful place, and I feel some envy for Claudette and Santi, and Dylan, who get to call this place home. Claudette followed her heart and moved from France to Portugal to be with her soulmate. It's all very romantic.

My phone buzzes and a text from Dylan appears on the screen:

Fancy a nightcap?

Mmm, I could do that. I type back:

Meet you at Santi's bar in an hour?

He replies quickly:

See you there

I can feel the grin on my face which instantly appeared as soon as Dylan's name flashed up on my phone, and I'm already looking forward to drinks. I finish my wine and eat, then quickly freshen up and touch up my makeup before setting off to meet Dylan.

Dylan is at the bar before me. As I approach, I can see him lounging on a white sofa chatting to Santi and I make my way over.

'Wow,' Dylan says as I stand opposite him, and I blush. 'You look hot.'

'Hey, Santi.' I turn to him. 'How are you?'

'I'm great, Kiera, thank you. Is that a new dress? Claudette said she had so much fun with you today.'

'We did have a good time, and yes, this is one of my many purchases.' I roll my eyes.

Santi laughs. 'Can I get you something to drink?'

I glance down at the glass in Dylan's hand. 'I'll have what he's having, please.'

'Of course.' Santi heads off into the bar and I sit down next to Dylan on the sofa.

He takes a sip from his glass. 'You have no idea what I'm drinking.'

'I'll take the risk. You had no idea what food I'd ordered when you intruded on my dinner.'

Dylan laughs. 'Very true.'

'Plus…' I take the glass from his hand. 'You don't seem like the terrible-drink type of person.' I take a drink from his glass and am pleasantly surprised to find it's refreshing and fruity.

'Gin and tonic? Really?'

'You're amused.' Dylan sits back in the sofa.

I nod. 'Yes.'

'Gin is very hip nowadays,' Dylan protests.

'I know.' I smirk.

'It's not a girlie drink. Gin is…' He stops as I'm laughing now, not at his gin drinking but at his protests of masculinity. He sighs loudly. 'Feel free to finish my gin.'

We spend the rest of the evening chatting, laughing, and of course drinking more gin. When we get up to leave, Dylan takes hold of my hand and we stroll across the square.

'How do you feel about mountains?' he asks as we walk.

'Um, I'm not sure. Why?'

'I thought tomorrow we could take a drive to Monchique. It's a fabulous little place, and you can go to the top of the mountain at Foia. The view is spectacular. On a clear day, you can see all the way to the Atlantic Ocean.'

‘Sounds interesting. I’d love to.’

‘I’ll pick you up at nine thirty. And bring your swimwear.’

‘To go up a mountain?’

‘No.’ Dylan smiles. ‘There’s a lovely cove we can go to afterwards. They have a great beach restaurant that serves the best mussels.’

I pull a face. ‘I’ve never tried mussels.’

‘Then you’re in for a treat.’

‘Yeah, I’m not so sure about that.’

‘Isn’t this whole Portugal trip about trying new things?’ Dylan reminds me.

‘I’ll consider it,’ I concede. ‘Right.’ I slide my hand from his as we reach the entrance to my apartment block. Dylan looks at me with a questioning expression. ‘Oh, you’re not coming up with me.’ I smile.

‘I’m not?’

‘No. See, we’re friends with benefits,’ I say in a faux-stern tone. ‘Tonight was an example of the friends part.’

Dylan shakes his head at me. ‘I told you that you were funny.’

I lean in and give him a kiss on the cheek. ‘Thank you for a lovely evening.’ I start to walk away.

‘So when do we get to do the benefits part?’

‘Goodnight, Dylan,’ I call over my shoulder. ‘See you tomorrow.’

I hear him chuckling as he walks away too.

As I get back into my apartment I congratulate myself on my powers of resistance. I could have very easily let Dylan come back up here and we could have had a repeat performance from a few nights ago, and what a performance it was. But I have to try to keep some equilibrium and not just fall head over heels and sleep with him every time we go out. We aren't a couple, this is not a relationship, this is – oh, I don't know what this is. I can try to convince myself that this is just a bit of fun, but in my heart I know that I'm falling for Dylan, and falling hard.

Chapter Nine

'I brought coffee,' Dylan says, handing me a takeaway mug as I climb into the car the following morning. I hope his driving is less erratic than Claudette's or I might end up wearing this. 'That's what friends do.' A grin pulls at the corners of his mouth.

'Thank you,' I say nonchalantly as I stare out of the window. 'Is it a long drive?'

'About an hour, but it'll be worth it, I promise.'

I take a drink of coffee. 'Perfect.'

We make small talk on the journey and we're at Monchique before we know it. Dylan parks up and we get out of the car and walk down the hill into the town. Dylan points out a number of historical sights, which yet again he seems to know far too much about, as we make our way to a local café.

'I thought we could go for a drink and have a *pastel de nata*, your favourite. I mean, you need to make sure you have plenty, given you travelled so far to have one,' Dylan says cheekily.

'Are you going to make fun of me the whole time?'

He shrugs. 'Not the whole time.'

After coffee and pastries, we drive up to Mount Foia. Dylan is right; the view is spectacular.

'This is the highest point of the Algarve,' Dylan says, as we stand and stare out at the incredible panoramic view. I have no idea how many miles you can see for, but it feels like I'm standing on top of the world.

I take a picture and send it to Gemma with the caption, *Love the view?* She loves stuff like this and would kill to be standing here with me (perhaps not when she's six months pregnant). I immediately get a text back: *So jealous. Looks amazing!! X*

'We should take a picture with the view in the background.'

'We, as in me and you?'

Dylan laughs softly. 'Well, that's usually what "we" means.'

'Right.' I hope he's not going to post this on social media. As I haven't told Gemma about my holiday companion yet, I could do without answering questions like, 'Who's the random man you're standing next to?'

Dylan stands closer to me, and I feel my heartbeat quicken as he rests his arm over my shoulders. This is so unhelpful. I do not need to have feelings for someone that firstly I've only just met, and secondly am not going to see again after the next few weeks. He leans in and I glance up at him and see that he's smiling widely at the phone. I follow his gaze and smile too. To everyone around we must look like a couple on holiday.

The phone clicks and Dylan inspects the photo. 'Perfect.' He shows me the phone and I look at the picture of us standing with the most incredible backdrop, both beaming.

'What are these all about?' I point to numerous small rock piles all around us.

Dylan shakes his head. 'I don't know.'

‘What do you mean, you don’t know? You know everything about every place we’ve been together.’

He shrugs. ‘Tourists make them. I don’t know why.’

We walk around and I take probably a hundred photographs covering every single angle of the view and numerous interesting rock piles.

‘Where are we going now then?’ I say, sliding my mobile phone back into my bag as we reach the car.

‘Well, we’ve done the mountain, and now we’re going to the secluded beach cove.’

‘That sounds very nice.’

We get into the car.

‘I mentioned it has a fabulous restaurant,’ Dylan says, ‘so we can grab dinner before we head home.’

‘It sounds perfect, minus the mussels that you also mentioned last night.’

He laughs. ‘There’s just one small hitch.’

I pull my sunglasses down my nose and turn to face Dylan. ‘What kind of hitch?’

He grins. ‘The journey is…how can I put it? A traditional Portuguese route, not usually for tourists.’

I don’t feel good about this. ‘What does that mean?’

Dylan chuckles and slides his sunglasses on. ‘It means, make sure your seatbelt is on.’

He accelerates and I take the advice, clipping in my seatbelt, and I push my sunglasses back up as we head left out of the car park at Foia and make our way further up the mountainside.

The scenery is stunning, and as I gaze out of the window I'm blown away by the beauty, the serenity, and the huge drop that's literally three inches away from my side of the car.

'What happens if a vehicle comes the other way?' I ask, instinctively leaning inwards towards the centre of the car, trying to change the centre of gravity as the road ahead seems to narrow, and it was already barely wide enough for one car.

'Calm down, will you. This is what driving in Portugal is like.'

'But why? This isn't a Third World country.'

Dylan laughs. ‘You act like I’m trying to kill you.’

‘Well, you just might be.’

‘You know, you…’

‘What?’

Dylan glances at me, then carries on watching the road.

‘Come on, what?’

‘Did I try to kill you when you came out on my boat?’

‘No.’

‘Well, you say that you are, your words not mine, boring and sensible, but you go out on a boat with a stranger – I mean, I wouldn’t say complete stranger; we had had dinner the night before.’

'You mean when you came and sat yourself down at my table and intruded on my personal time.'

'That's how you see that?'

'That's my recollection.'

'Well, I see…oh, uh-oh.'

'What?' I follow Dylan's gaze. 'Oh my God, there's a van coming the other way, there's a van.' I point through the windscreen at the approaching blue pickup.

'It's okay, there's plenty of room.'

'There's literally no room on my side, just a sheer drop off the side of the cliff.'

We edge closer to the cliff and I grip the seat tightly with both hands.

‘What are you doing?’ Dylan asks.

‘Holding on for dear life,’ I say, squeezing my eyes shut as the blue pickup squeezes past us. I don’t want to know how close to toppling over the edge I am.

Dylan laughs. ‘It’s okay. We’re past him. You can open your eyes.’

I glare at him accusingly. ‘This beach we’re heading to had better be worth it.’

Half an hour later I have to eat my words. As we descend down a small, dusty dirt track I see the glistening blue sea and golden sands. This is a slice of true paradise, and the death journey here was most definitely worth it. We climb out of the car, and I change into my flipflops before we make our way past the restaurant Dylan mentioned, which is painted crisp white and looks far too contemporary to be a beach café, and onto the sandy beach. As I slide onto a sunlounger and feel the sun beating down on me, I have to concede that today has been fantastic, death drive aside. Fabulous views from the top of the Foia mountains, and now I am on a secluded beach listening to the sounds of the sea.

I look at Dylan, lying on the lounger next to me, one arm raised above his head, causing his t-shirt to rise slightly and reveal ever such a tiny glimpse of his toned stomach. I touch his arm. He pulls down his sunglasses and rolls onto his side to face me.

'You okay?'

'Yes.' I nod. 'I just wanted to say thank you for today. I've really enjoyed it.'

He shrugs. ‘It’s not over yet.’

‘I know.’ I smile. ‘But I might forget to tell you later.’ I lie back down, close my eyes, and go back to listening to the rolling waves.

‘Cheers,’ I say as Dylan taps his wine glass against mine. His cheeks are sun-kissed from our afternoon lolling on loungers in this beautiful cove. The beach has quietened down, but the restaurant is busying up for the dinner rush. The smell of fresh fish cooking on the grill drifts in the air and I take a sip of the cold, crisp white wine.

‘This is the life.’ Dylan smiles across the table at me as he sips his own wine. We’ve just ordered fresh lobster from the menu, which I would never in a million years have ordered before, and I’m a little scared of how on earth I'm going to eat it when it arrives at the table, although it's far preferable to attempting to eat mussels.

I frown at him curiously. 'Yeah, it is. So how have you ended up living it?'

'What do you mean?'

'How have you found all of these places?'

'I do live here, you know, and I don't work every minute of every day.'

'So you spend the rest of the time doing what? Eating shrimp and drinking wine at nice restaurants on your own?'

Dylan pauses, his wine glass nearly at his lips. 'Oh, right. I see where this is going. You think I'm some sort of gigolo, taking a different woman to a different place every time.'

'Gigolo?' I raise my eyebrows.

'A ladies' man. Swooping in on women and plying them with wine and nice food in return for…?'

I suck in my cheeks. When he puts it like that, it sounds awful.

'You're wrong. I'm not that guy.'

I tap my wine glass.

'Not in the slightest.'

'How come you're sitting here with me?'

'I'm sure it sounds very corny, but I told you this: I like you.'

'Why do you like me?'

'Because you're different.'

'How am I different?'

He pauses a moment before answering. 'I don't know. Maybe if I could tell you, then we wouldn't be sitting here.' He sips his wine. 'You ask a lot of questions.'

'No, *you* ask a lot of questions.'

Dylan chuckles. 'Because you don't like talking about yourself. Why?'

'I've never said that.'

'You don't have to. Your body language says it all. Crossed arms, frowning, instinctively defensive.'

I hadn't realised that my arms were folded; I hadn't consciously done that. I can feel that my brow is furrowed and I try to relax my facial muscles while discretely sliding my arms to my sides.

'So you wouldn't call yourself a risk taker?' Dylan says.

'I most definitely would *not* call myself a risk taker.'

He looks at me, his head cocked to one side. 'Why do you think that is?'

'I don't know.'

'Sure you do.'

I'm not used to divulging personal information to anyone; sometimes I even keep Gemma at arm's length. I've always been a kind of 'keep it all in and carry on' type of girl.

'I'm not comfortable talking about my feelings.'

'With me?'

'With anyone.'

'Why do you think that is?'

I smile. 'If I answer, then wouldn't that be me talking about my feelings?'

Dylan raises his eyebrows at me, and silence hangs between us.

I take a sip from my wine glass. 'I don't like talking about my feelings. I feel weak and vulnerable when I do, so I choose not to.'

'You're more the strong and silent type.'

‘It works for me.’

‘I always thought that was a guy thing, keeping everything inside.’

‘Some women do that too.’

‘You’re fooling no-one.’ Dylan shakes his head. ‘Look, you don’t want to talk about yourself much, that’s fine.’ He shrugs. ‘But maybe you should ask yourself why. I’m not buying this vulnerable stuff. You’re here on your own. That doesn’t sound like a vulnerable person to me.’

‘I just don’t like talking about myself.’

‘That’s not a reason.’

‘Maybe I don’t have anything interesting to say.’

‘I don’t believe that, Kiera, and all the time we’ve spent together tells me the opposite.’

'You should ask my ex. He would confirm it. We never did anything exciting, anything really…memorable.'

'He sounds like a jerk.'

I tip my head to one side. 'No, not really. It wasn't his fault.'

'What wasn't his fault?'

'We were both the same; that was the problem. We were both too sensible, too bothered about doing things the right way, not taking risks, doing what people expected of us.'

'What people?'

I shrug. 'Our parents, I guess.'

'How come?'

'They had both grown up in the same town, left school, got a job, bought a house, got married, had children.'

'So at which point in the list were you? Are you married?' He looks at me, wide-eyed.

'No, I'm not married.'

'Didn't think so.' He shakes his head.

'I don't look like the marrying type?' I'm officially offended.

'More that you wouldn't suit a meringue.'

I have to agree, I probably wouldn't.

My heart sinks. 'Are *you* married?'

Dylan laughs, shaking his head again. 'Definitely not married.'

'Long-term girlfriend?' I ask nervously. Perhaps I should have asked this *before* I slept with him.

He looks away slightly before answering. 'No, not right now.'

'Sounds like there has been.' I take a sip of my fabulous wine.

'Not really, no.'

I raise my eyebrows, amused. 'Hmm, commitment-phobe?'

'I see what you're doing here.'

'Really and what's that?' I say coyly.

'Deflecting the questions away from you and putting them onto me.'

The waiter interrupts our exchange as he places a huge lobster down on the table between us. I stare at it with a mixture of fear and anticipation.

Dylan grins. 'Allow me,' he says as he dives in.

It's a messy affair, but I think lobster might just be my new favourite food.

The drive home takes us on a scenic route down the coastline. As I look out at the idyllic views my eyelids feel heavy. Words of conversation are few and far between, and as I see a sign saying we're ten kilometres from home, I stifle a yawn.

'Do you have any plans tonight?' Dylan asks.

'Other than calling my best friend, Gemma, and having an early night, no.'

'Fair enough. I can take the hint. Today has been enough excitement for you.'

'I am feeling tired. I think it's my body adjusting to the heat and things – maybe the interrogation over lobster and wine.'

Dylan appears to choose to ignore that last comment.

As we pull into my apartment complex, Dylan says, 'I have a busy day with work tomorrow and a late client meeting, but we could meet for breakfast the following morning.'

'Let's do that.'

'Vilamoura again? At the same place as last time?'

'I don't need asking twice to go where there's amazing coffee and chocolate croissants.'

'Nine thirty suit you?'

'See you then.'

'Wait.' Dylan puts his hand over mine as I go to get out of the car. 'We did the friends thing yesterday, so I think it's only right that we do the benefits thing today.'

I look him straight in the eye. 'And what did you have in mind?'

'Seeing as you're having a night to yourself, I guess we'll have to make do with this.' He leans in and kisses me passionately, so much so that I'm weak at the knees and struggle to climb out of the car as we part company.

I walk into the apartment in a slight daze, a mix of tiredness and adrenaline from the kiss. I make a cup of tea and pick up my phone to call Gemma.

She answers the phone after two rings. 'Hey, how are you, stranger?'

'It's only been two days since we last spoke, Gemma.'

She huffs. 'It feels much longer because you're so far away.'

'I'm in Europe, not Australia,' I retort jokingly.

'Are you having fun?'

'Yes, it's lovely here. I've been shopping with Claudette, you know, who owns the bar.'

'Oh, yes, you mentioned her. Do they have nice clothes out there?'

‘I’ve spent a small fortune,’ I confess.

‘What about that really hot guy you bumped into? Have you seen him again?’

‘Um, kind of.’

‘Kiera.’ I can hear her tone change.

‘I’ve just been, um, spending some time with him. We’ve become friends.’ I leave out the ‘with benefits’ part.

‘You’re having a holiday romance now?’

I frown, not realising that Gemma can’t actually see me. I’ve stuck to my promise to myself not to video-call. ‘It’s not a holiday romance. I’m not on holiday; it’s a sabbatical.’

‘Which is a posh way of saying “taking a break”, i.e. a holiday, and that’s not what I asked.’

'He's just helping me to see more of the place, that's all, showing me around.'

'I bet he is.'

'It's not like these things have a long-term perspective.'

'What things?'

'Holiday romances.'

'I thought it wasn't a holiday romance.'

'Well, it's not like I slept with him so now I think we're going to live happily ever after.'

'Hang on a minute. You slept with him?' Gemma's tone is bordering on one that only dogs can hear.

Shit. Why did I admit to that? Why?

'It was a minor indiscretion. I got carried away in the moment,' I say defensively.

'Oh.'

'You're judging me.'

'Not judging you. It's just so…not like you, that's all.'

'See, this is what happens, Gem, when you go off for a month to another country in complete contrast to your usual boring…'

'You're never boring.'

'…sensible self. You do unpredictable things like sleeping with some random hot guy with a boat.'

'So he's definitely hot?'

'Maybe.'

‘He has a boat! OMG!’

‘Maybe.’

‘Is it a big, um, boat?’

I suck in my cheeks. ‘Now you’re just being rude.’

Gemma giggles.

‘And childish, so I’m going to hang up.’

‘Wait, Kiera.’

I press the ‘end call’ button. Hmm, that didn’t go well, did it, Kiera? You confessed all to Gemma, in fact not all, just all of the bad bits, and you added no context to it. Although what the context is, I’m not entirely sure.

Chapter Ten

I drive to Vilamoura to meet Dylan for breakfast, a whole thirty six hours since I got out of his car, and I park next to the marina again. As I walk through to where the restaurant is, I can already see Dylan sitting at a table on the decking overlooking the water. He's not in his usual crisp white shirt and navy shorts; today he's in a navy shirt and chinos, and if possible, he looks even sexier in this attire.

'I took the liberty of ordering,' Dylan says as I take a seat opposite him.

'Thank you.' I stare out at the water below as a huge fish pops up to the surface. 'It's a lovely morning. Does it ever rain here?'

'Not much in the summer months, and only occasionally in the winter months. You can get a cold rolling fog in winter, which isn't much fun, but it's not cold like the UK is cold.'

'Mmm, I could get used to a warmer climate. No more de-icing the car before setting off for work in the mornings. No more gale-force wind whipping around your face in December while you Christmas-shop.'

'Ah, I remember those days – the weather in the UK, not the Christmas shopping.' He grins.

'Of course not. You're a man,' I say, rolling my eyes at him.

'I would be offended by your clearly sexist and provocative comment, but –'

'I'm right,' I say, satisfied.

‘Someone didn’t invent the internet for nothing, you know. Online shopping is a thing.’

‘You don’t get the same experience, though, as with actual shopping.’

‘No, and I hear you like the whole experience.’

I grit my teeth. ‘Claudette has a lot to answer for.’

The waitress, not Cassie this time, brings over our coffee and croissants, and we dig in.

‘Do you ever just lie back and look up at the stars?’ Dylan asks, licking the remaining croissant crumbs from his fingertips, and I watch him, mesmerised.

‘Er, no.’

'Okay, tonight we're going to the beach and we're going to sit on the sand and you're going to look up at the stars and you'll know exactly what I mean.'

'Tonight? As in, when it's dark?'

Dylan half smiles. 'That's usually when the stars appear.'

'How will I see where I'm going?'

'You have a mobile phone, don't you?'

'You know I do.'

'Then it has a torch button.'

'Oh, yes.'

'And you'll be with me. I won't let anything happen to you. You trust me, don't you?'

I look up at him, smiling. ‘I don’t know. I haven’t quite decided yet.’

‘Do I need to tell Claudette where we’re going again so you know I’m not a serial killer?’ he says playfully.

I shake my head. ‘No, I trust that you aren’t a serial killer.’

‘Glad that’s sorted. We might as well have dinner together first.’

I smile coyly. ‘I can do dinner, but only if you agree to go to the Italian place – I haven’t tried there yet.’

‘I’ll meet you there at seven thirty p.m.’ His phone beeps and he scowls at the screen. ‘But now I must go and actually do some work. See you tonight.’

'Dylan,' I call as he walks away. He stops and turns back around. 'I'm not going to regret this, am I?'

'Life is too short for regrets, Kiera.' Dylan chuckles as he turns back around and then he disappears from sight.

Life is too short for regrets? Is that true? There's many a thing that I regret.

I spend the afternoon lazing by the pool, making a promise to do some sightseeing tomorrow and not spend the entire time here in Portugal horizontal on a sunlounger. The temptation to do so is very strong given the glorious sunshine and the peaceful surroundings. Again, there's only a handful of people, also horizontal on sunloungers, around the pool. I put in my headphones and select 'Ibiza Chilled' from my music selection, and I lie back and close my eyes, tapping my foot to the soft beat.

Shit, what time is it? I sit up so quickly that my sunglasses take a dive to the left from the sudden movement and land on the ground for the second time since I arrived here, and I squint into the low orange sunlight. The music on my phone must have ended a long time ago. I press the screen on my phone. Six forty-five p.m. Damn, I need to be showered, dressed, and at the restaurant to meet Dylan by seven thirty.

I scoop my sunglasses off the ground and fling my towel and phone into my beach bag at the side of the lounger. I shiver, slipping my feet into my red-hot flipflops, and hurry back to the apartment block, where I take the stairs two at a time – there's no time to wait for that slow lift.

Once inside the apartment, I unload my towel and bag in the kitchen and begin undressing on my way to the bathroom, discarding my bikini on the floor as I go. Turning on the shower, I climb in.

'Argh!'

And then immediately hop back out.

Glancing in the mirror, I see a slightly-pinker-than-expected reflection greeting me.

Bloody hell!

I lean cautiously into the shower and adjust the water temperature to barely warm, then take a deep breath before climbing back in. It's possibly the quickest shower in history as I battle with shower gel and shampoo whilst trying at all costs to stop water from hitting my skin. I decide to abandon blow-drying my hair and opt for air-drying and leave-in conditioning spray instead. The heat in the apartment is enough to air-dry my hair without too much effort.

I lather on freezing-cold aloe vera lotion, which seems to ignite the heat in my sunburned skin rather than douse it, and apply the appropriate amount of makeup to cover the pink tinge on my face without turning myself into a clown. A swish of pink lip gloss and a swift pull through my hair with hair straighteners, and I decide that will have to do as I have minus three minutes to get to the Italian restaurant.

I slip on my comfy wedges and pull on a navy maxi dress, hoping the plain dark colour will minimise my red skin. Grabbing a small, cross-body handbag, I head back out of the apartment and into the warm evening.

I can see Dylan on my approach to the restaurant, sitting at a table, sunglasses on, drinking a glass of red wine.

'Sorry I'm late,' I say as I walk up to the table. 'I was…'

He cocks his head to one side and smiles. 'Falling asleep in the sun?'

'Don't joke about it.' I sit down gingerly, feeling embarrassment flush my already flushed cheeks.

'You need to stay out of the sun for a day or two.' He takes a sip of wine before placing his glass back down on the table and picking up the wine bottle and filling my glass. 'This might help take the sting out of it.'

'Really?'

'No.' He shakes his head. 'But it's nice wine, and we're having dinner, so make sure you drink plenty of water tomorrow.'

'Fair enough.' I pick up the glass and take a gulp. 'Mmm, this is really nice wine.'

'I love this wine. It's made here in Portugal, in the Alentejo region. We should go wine tasting while you're here.'

'That sounds like a good way to spend a day. I'll drink to that.' I giggle and clink my glass against his.

The waiter comes and takes our order and our conversation resumes.

‘Are we really going to sit on the beach in the dark and look up at the stars later?’

‘Absolutely.’

‘And you’ve done this how many times before?’

‘Hundreds.’

I nod sceptically.

‘I promise, you’ll feel a total sense of relaxation.’

‘I’m prepared to give it a go, only because I feel that I’m not going to hear the last of it if I don’t.’

‘Duly noted.’ Dylan chuckles.

'Okay,' I concede. I turn my head to face Dylan. 'You're right, this is amazing. The stars look so clear and bright, and there's millions of them. I can't believe how beautiful it is.'

I'm met with silence.

'Dylan.'

He holds up one hand.

'What?'

'I'm just enjoying this moment of being right.'

I slap his arm playfully.

'I can't believe you haven't done this in every place that you've been,' he says.

'Well, for a start, I would have had to have been to many places.'

Dylan pushes himself up onto his elbows. 'You haven't travelled much?'

I shake my head. 'Not so much.'

'How come?'

I think back to the girls' holidays that I had with Gemma, before she and Tom got married. They were few and far between, and usually consisted of a drunken week in Ibiza where we were in a nightclub by the time the stars made an appearance.

'Whatever the reason, I plan to change that. I've got the travel bug, I think, and I love the sun.'

'It's a different pace of life here,' Dylan says, staring back up at the stars.

'Yeah, and you get to see the sky looking like this.'

We lie there quietly, both staring at the starry sky above.

‘Kiera,’ Dylan says.

‘Yes.’

‘Do you want to get out of here?’ he asks.

I play along. ‘And go where?’

‘To my apartment. Because I want you right now, and if we make love here, who knows where sand could end up?’

I burst out laughing at this and Dylan pulls me towards him, kissing me hard, and I want him here and now too. He pulls me to my feet and takes me by the hand, and I follow him eagerly.

Dylan rests his chin on my stomach. 'You're amazing, you know that, and beautiful.'

I laugh shyly and don't quite meet his gaze.

'What? I'm not allowed to pay you a compliment?' He reaches up and brushes my cheek with his thumb. 'Why do you look embarrassed when I say something nice about you?'

'I don't know.' I shrug.

Dylan cocks his head to one side.

'Okay, so maybe I'm not used to someone saying that I'm amazing.'

'And beautiful.'

I feel my cheeks blush crimson.

'Your other boyfriends, they didn't compliment you? Not that I'm your boyfriend.'

I press my lips together.

'You seem dismissive, like you don't want to take a compliment.'

'Are you too good to be true?' The words are out of my mouth before I can engage my brain.

Dylan chuckles. 'Too good to be true?'

'You know, like people always say: if something seems too good to be true, then it probably is.'

He laughs loudly at this.

'So this is funny? You find me funny?'

He rolls over and sits up, pulling the covers up to his waist. 'What I think is funny is that your response to somebody saying something nice to you is to assume they're lying, what, to get you into bed?' He raises his eyebrows and whispers, 'We already did that. Twice.' He holds up two fingers.

'I didn't mean…' I falter. I'm not sure what I meant.

'Yes, you did, but that's okay. You, miss, are an introvert who is emotionally…' A smile plays on his lips. '…guarded.'

I nod begrudgingly. 'I guess that's fair.'

'And I wear my heart and my emotions on my sleeve. I tell it how I see it, no agenda.'

'I guess you do.'

'Which I'm not ashamed of. Life is too short to waver, to beat about the bush. If I like something, or someone, then I go for it, one hundred per cent.'

I don't know if it's the fact that I'm lying here, naked, vulnerable, being told that I'm amazing and beautiful by someone who's probably the hottest guy I've ever laid naked with, but I feel incredibly turned on.

'I'm sorry,' I whisper.

'That's okay.' Dylan feigns a hurt look. 'I know how you can make it up to me.'

'Next time you pay me a compliment, I'll say thank you.'

He moves under the covers and sits, straddling me. 'I had something else in mind.'

Chapter Eleven

Wow, that sun is bright. I can already feel the warmth on my face as sunlight streaks through the crack where the curtains meet.

Hang on a minute.

The bedroom in the apartment has blinds at the window, not curtains.

I roll over gently, somewhat relieved to find myself in an empty bed, in Dylan's empty bed.

I roll up to a seated position and flashbacks of last night flow freely through my mind – dinner, lovely Italian food, lots of lovely Italian wine. A stroll along the beach, lying on the sand and gazing up at the stars, mesmerised.

Coming back to Dylan's apartment.

Making love.

Falling asleep in his arms.

Dylan is not in the bedroom. Is he somewhere else in the apartment?

This is déjà vu. But this time, I pull the covers back over me and wait for Dylan to reappear with coffee and pastries. A few moments later I hear the front door open, and Dylan appears at the bedroom door.

'Good morning,' he says, smiling broadly at me. 'I brought breakfast. I don't know about you, but I'm starving. We burned off quite a few calories last night.'

We eat breakfast and then I head back to my apartment. I change into my swimsuit, throw a towel, sunscreen, a large bottle of chilled water, and a crime thriller paperback into an oversized beach bag, and head to the pool. It's fairly quiet, just a couple of other sunbathers hiding behind sunglasses and sunhats. I choose a lounger in the far corner, away from everyone, and make myself comfy under a huge umbrella, careful to sit in the shade after baking in the sun yesterday.

I rub my eyes groggily. So much for feeling refreshed on this break. Looking at my phone, I realise that it's half past one. I need caffeine, in large quantities. Portuguese coffee may be the best that I've tasted, but what's with the tiny cups?

Coffee should come in a large mug. I grab my bag and head back up to the apartment to make lunch and get a caffeine fix.

Sitting down with a large coffee and a chicken salad baguette, I see a new text message flashing in my inbox. I take a bite of my sandwich. It's probably Gemma wanting her daily update on my whereabouts. Honestly, she worries about me more than my own mother. But when I click on the text, it's not from Gemma. My breath catches in my throat.

I miss you, reads the text, from an unknown number.

It takes me a couple of seconds staring at the screen to recognise the number. It's one that I used to know. That was in my phone and used daily. But

I deleted it when Jacob walked out the door and we called time on our relationship, and now I get this, *I miss you.* What does that even mean, apart from the obvious literal translation? He misses me? He was the one who ended things.

I toss the phone to the end of the table and carry on eating, but as I swallow, the food sticks in my throat. As I gulp at my coffee, I hear the distinct ping from my smartphone, announcing a new text.

I stare at the phone at the end of the table like it's an unexploded bomb. Well, maybe it is. Who knows what that ping will reveal? It might not be from Jacob. It could just be from Gemma.

I bite my lip. What the hell. I'm going to have to look; whether I do it now or sit here like an idiot for another ten minutes, it's not going to change the outcome. I scoop up the phone and stare at the screen.

We made a mistake. I made a mistake. I got complacent. I took you for granted, took us for granted. I should have made more effort. I should have romanced you more. I'm sorry.

My hand trembles as I read the text over and over. Then the phone pings again.

I want you back. I want us back. I love you.

Whoa.

I blink three times, then look back at the screen on the phone. Yep. I didn't imagine it. The words are still there: *I want us back. I love you.*

I launch the phone and it skids across the table and lands with a sickening crunch on the tiled balcony, which will no doubt cost me the equivalent of a month's rent to fix despite the fact that these phones are supposed to be invincible nowadays. This is serious. And there's only one person who can help me. I collect the phone from the floor, which thankfully seems to have survived, and I hit speed dial one in my phonebook.

'Okay, don't overreact.'

'Why would I overreact?' Gemma's voice reaches a high note that shouldn't come out of a human being. 'What have you done now?'

'Nothing! And I'm going to ignore that inference.'

'Just spill it.'

'I got a text.'

‘From?’

‘From Jacob.’

‘Whoa.’

‘That’s what I said.’

‘Well, what did it say?’

‘I want you back.’

‘He wants you back?’

‘He says he should have made more of an effort, and he took us, me, for granted.’

‘And he wants you back?’

‘That’s what he says.’

‘Do you want *him* back?’

I pause, just for a second, but it’s a second too long and Gemma pounces.

'You want him back, Kiera?'

I hold the mobile phone away from my ear before she can do any further damage to my eardrum. 'I didn't say that.'

'But you didn't say that you don't.'

'Fair point.'

'So?'

'Oh, I don't know. No, yes, maybe. No. Definitely no.'

'Who are you trying to convince? Because I really hope that it's not me.'

'It's complicated.'

'No, it isn't. Do you still have feelings for him?'

‘Of course. We spent four years of our lives together. But I can’t go backwards.’

‘This isn’t a new strategy you’ve implemented at work, Kiera. We’re talking about a relationship.’

‘I know that.’

‘And it’s not going backwards if two people who still have feelings for each other realise that they’ve made a mistake and get back together.’

‘I didn’t say I was considering getting back together with Jacob.’

‘But you are considering it, or we wouldn’t be having this conversation.’

Damn it. Gemma is right. Am I really considering getting back with Jacob?

‘What’s that?’ Gemma says.

'The apartment buzzer.'

'Who is it?'

'I don't know.'

'Well, go and see.'

I hold the phone to my chest and walk over to the intercom. 'Hello?'

'It's only me.'

'Oh, come up.' I press the door release.

'Okay, I'm back,' I say into the mobile phone.

'Who was it?'

'Dylan.'

'Dylan as in the hot guy you've been hanging out with?'

I gulp. 'That would be the one.'

‘Of course. The foreign lover. You’ve just got them queuing up for you.’

‘He’s not foreign; he’s English. He just lives in Portugal.’

‘Same thing.’

There’s knocking at the door now, signalling Dylan’s arrival.

‘I don’t have time for this. I need to go, Gemma. I’ll call you later.’

‘Kiera?’

I hang up the phone and open the door.

‘Hey, are you okay?’ Dylan says. ‘You look a little flustered.’

I smile. ‘I’m fine, just couldn’t get someone off the phone.’

'Anything important?'

'Just a sales call,' I lie.

The sand is warm between my toes as we stroll along the beach a short while later.

'Are you hungry?' Dylan asks.

'A little.'

'I'll be back in a second.'

He leaves me standing there as he jogs further along the sand and approaches a man carrying two large cooler boxes. They chat for a minute before the guy hands him two paper bags and Dylan jogs back to me. He's grinning as he holds out a bag towards me.

'Bola de Berlim.'

'A what now?'

'You'll love it, I promise.'

I take the bag sceptically and unfold the opening. 'It's a donut.'

Dylan rolls his eyes at me. 'This isn't *just* a donut. This is the nicest donut you'll ever taste. It's soft and sugary with the lightest custard filling.'

'It's huge.'

'I'm sure you'll manage.' Dylan chuckles as he opens his own bag and takes a bite.

I follow suit. 'Oh my God, that's amazing,' I say through a mouthful of the most delicious thing I have ever tasted. 'I'll be going back to England a stone heavier at this rate.' I glance over at him as he takes another bite of his own *bola de whatever*.

'How are you not a stone overweight with all the food you've sampled and introduced me to since I got here? You eat cake or pastry at least once every day.'

Dylan stops mid-bite. 'That's a little personal, don't you think?'

'Really, you think that's a bit personal? I've seen you naked.'

'I have a fast metabolism.'

'Lucky you. I have to work off every cake that I eat.'

Dylan grins. 'Great, want to eat another donut, then we can head back to yours to work them both off?'

I raise my eyebrows at him. 'I thought it wasn't just a donut.'

Dylan laughs. 'That wasn't a no.'

Dylan leaves my apartment a few hours later for a client meeting and I decide to go for a drive to clear my head. I'm thankful that he is working on a project tomorrow with a tight deadline, so we won't get chance to meet. Dylan was a nice distraction this afternoon from Jacob's texts, but now that he's gone, those texts are on repeat in my head. I climb in the car and start driving. I don't know where I'm heading, I just drive.

I end up, some time later, at a remote beach café at the end of a dusty track that in all honestly I was regretting driving down. There's a handful of people sitting at tables. I take a seat overlooking the sea and order a glass of wine. The waiter brings it and I tap the stem of the glass as I watch the waves roll in. This truly is a beautiful part of the world.

I take a sip and think back to my conversation with Gemma. Do I still love Jacob? Would rekindling our relationship be going backwards? If I don't consider it, will I regret it?

I take another drink of wine. If I'm being truthful, really truthful, I *do* still love Jacob. I always did. That's why when he suggested we broke up, I slept on the sofa bed, letting him stay, secretly hoping that he would change his mind. I try to make out that our relationship was boring, but the reality is that it was comfortable, and relaxed, and easy.

So what now, Kiera?

I stare out at the beach. It's pretty empty, so I drink the remainder of my wine, leave the money on the table, and walk down onto the sand. I take my flipflops off and walk into the surf. The water is cold as it swirls around my feet and I exhale deeply. What am I doing here? Experiencing new things, or running away from them?

Things with Dylan have moved really fast, and it's been great. He's made me feel attractive, and fun, and free. But maybe we need to slow things down and I need to take a bit of time out to get my head straight.

My mobile phone rings and I reach for it in my bag. I stare at the number on the screen before answering.

'Hi,' says a familiar voice on the other end of the phone.

My breath catches in my throat and I swallow, but it does nothing to dislodge the large ball of cotton wool that appears to have squashed itself into my mouth. I try, and fail, to speak.

Jacob clears his throat. 'I know, you probably weren't expecting my call.'

'Yes. No. Um.' Not only do I not recognise the voice that's come out of me, but I also seem incapable of making any sense.

'I shouldn't have sent you those texts.'

Oh, great. So now he has buyer's remorse.

'I should have waited until I saw you in person, but I went by your house a couple of times, and you weren't in.'

He went to my house. Maybe he is serious about wanting me back. I cough, dislodging the cotton wool ball.

'I'm not in.'

'So when might you be home? I was thinking we could talk things through over a bottle of red. I've got a bottle of that Pinot Noir that you love.'

I smile, sadly, happily, I don't know. 'That sounds nice, but like I said, I'm not home.'

'So when will you be…home?'

I glance down at the sea still lapping against my ankles. 'Um, I'm in Portugal.'

I hear the small intake of breath down the phone.

'Oh.'

'It was a bit of an impulse thing,' I splutter, although why I feel the need to justify myself, I have no idea. 'I just wanted to get away.'

There's a pause before Jacob speaks. 'I'm sorry if I made you feel that way. I can't believe how stupid I've been. Maybe it took our being apart for me to realise how much you mean to me, how great we were together.'

My heart tightens.

'Say something, Kiera, please.'

I shake my head. 'I don't know what to say.'

'Do you still love me?'

I swallow. ‘That’s not a simple question to answer.’

‘For me it is. I love you, Kiera. I want you back. When can I see you?’

‘I’m home the week after next,’ I say quietly.

‘And we can meet then?’

‘I guess so.’ The words are out of my mouth before I can think any further.

I hear the relief in Jacob’s voice as he says, ‘That’s great, Kiera. Thank you. I can’t wait to see you. Bye.’

I hang up the phone and stand in the sea for a while longer, contemplating what I’ve just done, but as I walk back up the sand towards the car, I still have no idea if it was the right thing.

Chapter Twelve

I've been ignoring Dylan's calls and texts for several days now. I've avoided the square and the restaurants and bars in it in a lame effort to avoid bumping into him. The conversation with Jacob has sent me spinning. I used retail therapy as a distraction, but that failed, so I hiked up God knows what cliffside to take in the views, but that didn't work either. Now I find myself nursing an espresso in a small coffee shop in the next town along, still in hiding.

'Kiera?'

I jump, looking up from my coffee, to find Claudette standing next to my table with her usual broad smile.

'Hi,' I say sheepishly.

'How are you? I have not seen you around.'

'Oh, yeah, I've been sightseeing and stuff,' I say, hopefully convincingly.

'Oh, that's good. I thought you had hated the food or something, no?'

'Oh, of course not. Your food is fabulous.'

Claudette points to the chair opposite me. 'May I?'

'Sure.' I smile.

'Café, por favor,' Claudette says to a passing waitress before she takes a seat at the table. 'Are you going to tell me what is actually going on?'

'What do you mean?'

'We have not seen you around. Dylan has been asking after you. He is worried, yes?'

‘He has nothing to worry about.’ I shrug. ‘I’m fine.’

The waitress places an espresso on the table in front of Claudette. She takes a sip as we sit there in silence. After a minute or two, I speak.

‘My ex-boyfriend, he contacted me.’

Claudette looks at me with a blank expression and waits for me to go on.

‘He says that he still loves me and he wants me back.’

‘Ah.’ She nods. ‘And you don’t feel the same?’

‘I don’t know. Maybe.’

‘Maybe? You know how you feel in your heart, Kiera. Be honest with yourself.’

Wow, Claudette definitely doesn't beat about the bush.

'I do still have feelings for him,' I say.

'So this is why you are avoiding Dylan?'

'I didn't say that I was avoiding him.'

Claudette just looks at me.

'I might have made myself unavailable to Dylan over the last few days.'

'Why would you do that? This guy is your life back home, yes? You say that you and Dylan are…what did you say, a four-week thing?'

'I did say that.'

'And things have now changed?'

‘And things have now changed.’ I drink my espresso. Jesus, that’s strong.

‘You love Dylan, yes?’

I cough awkwardly. ‘I’m not sure that love is the right word, but –’

Claudette frowns at me. ‘You have feelings for Dylan.’

I tap the table. ‘Yes,’ I agree. ‘I have feelings for Dylan.’

‘You cannot avoid him for the rest of your time here.’

Can’t I? No, no, I can’t.

‘You need to be honest with him, Kiera. Dylan deserves that much,’ Claudette says, standing up to leave.

I look at her, then nod. I know that she's right, and unfortunately for me, she's saying the same thing as my conscience, which I've been trying to ignore for the last few days too.

I head back to my apartment and emergency-call Gemma.

'Okay, don't freak out,' is my opening line.

'Why would I freak out?'

'Gemma.'

'Of course I won't freak out.'

I exhale slowly. 'Jacob called me.'

'What?!'

'You're freaking out.'

'No. No, I'm not. I'm just…surprised. Please go on.'

'He called me to say sorry. He wants us to have a drink together when I get back.'

'What? Why?'

I don't answer.

'Oh my God, he definitely wants you to get back together, doesn't he?'

I shrug and stare out of the window, regretting having this conversation now. It could have waited until I got back to the UK. Gemma is always less confrontational face to face.

'You think that would be a bad idea?' I ask her.

'Don't you?'

'I don't know.'

'Are you saying that because you want to get back together with Jacob, or…'

'Or?'

'Or…are you panicking because you're turning thirty-two and you're single?'

'Huh. That would be insulting if it came from anyone, but coming from my best friend, it really hurts.'

'Kiera, look, I didn't mean that the way it came out.'

'Really? Are there other ways to say that you think that I'm sad and lonely, and over the hill at thirty-one?'

'That's not what I meant. It's just that, you know, you split up with Jacob and then flew to another country for a month.'

'Yes, to have a change of scenery, to experience new things, to sit on a beach with a book and relax, for God's sake. I'm not having an early mid-life crisis!' My voice has raised a few octaves and I don't know who's more shocked by that, Gemma or me.

'Okay, okay, calm down. I'm sorry. Can we move past my stupid comment, please?'

I huff. 'Okay.'

'Let's go back to Jacob then. What did he say?'

'He said he was sorry, that he should have made more effort, and…and that he misses me.'

'Do you miss him?'

'If I'm honest, then yes, I do miss him. We had some good times together. Maybe we should give it a second chance. Everybody has to work at their relationship, and maybe we took each other for granted.'

'Hmm.'

'You don't sound convinced.'

'It's not me who needs to be,' Gemma says. 'Are you convinced?'

'I don't know, but I think I want to find out.'

'Then there's your answer. Go for a drink with him. Hear what he has to say. See how you feel when you're right there in front of him. Trust your gut.'

'Yeah?'

'Yeah.'

'Gemma, we both know that my gut will tell me to do the most sensible thing.'

'Well, only you can decide if that's walking away from Jacob forever or taking another chance with him.'

I end the call with Gemma, and then, before I can back out of my decision, I text Dylan:

Sorry I've been out of the picture. Are you free for dinner tonight?

I stare at the phone, willing it to beep, signalling a new text, but nothing. I guess I deserve that.

An hour later, I'm still staring at my phone when it beeps loudly and a text from Dylan appears on the screen. My stomach knots as I reach for my phone and click on the message:

Santi's at 8pm?

I quickly text back: *See you there.*

I place the phone down on the coffee table and walk out onto the balcony. I stand, watching people below as they wander down to the pool or off to the beach. It feels like I've been here for a long time, but at the same time I can't believe that I go home in just over a week.

The afternoon drags, and I watch every second tick by on the clock until it's time to meet Dylan for dinner. As I walk to Santi's, I feel nervous about seeing Dylan. As per usual, he's already sitting there, glass of wine in his hand, as I approach.

'Well, hello, stranger,' he says coyly as I hover next to the table.

'Hi,' I reply meekly, unsure of his mood.

Dylan gestures to the chair across the table from him. 'Are you going to sit down?'

'Yes.' I roll my eyes, sitting down opposite him.

We lock eyes.

'Wine?' Dylan keeps his gaze right on me as he picks up the bottle of red next to him and pours me a glass.

I take a sip, grateful for the moment to collect myself, and also the hit of alcohol. I decide to take the direct approach and get it over with.

'I owe you an apology,' I say, diverting my gaze downwards.

'For what?'

Okay, so he's not going to let me off lightly.

'I was avoiding you.'

Dylan nods. 'I nearly came over to your apartment a number of times,' he says. 'Just to make sure you were still alive.'

'Right,' I respond. I don't know what else to say.

'But then Claudette told me that she saw you having coffee, so I knew that you were safe and well.'

'Yes.'

'And that it was clear that you didn't want to see me.'

I take a deep breath. 'It's not that simple.'

'Explain it to me.' He takes a gulp of wine and looks at me, waiting for my response.

'Things between us were moving quickly,' I start, 'and I was enjoying that.'

'But?'

'But we agreed this would be…I don't know.' I shake my head. 'More casual than it's become.'

Dylan nods but says nothing.

'My ex-boyfriend called me,' I blurt out, and Dylan flinches, before composing himself.

'Hey, you two. Are you having food tonight?' Claudette breaks the glass wall between us as she places menus down on the table.

'Hi, Claudette.' I smile at her. Dylan is still staring at me in silence. 'We might just need a minute,' I say.

She looks from Dylan to me and smiles warmly. 'Of course. I will come back.'

As she walks away, Dylan speaks. 'I'm not sure what your ex-boyfriend calling you means.'

'Me neither.' I take another drink of wine.

'Does he want you back?' Dylan fiddles with his wine glass.

'That's what he says,' I confirm.

'And do you want to get back with him?'

I press my lips together. 'We said this was just a four-week thing – friends with benefits.'

Dylan nods. 'Right.'

I swallow nervously. ‘It felt like it was becoming more than that.’

Dylan licks his lips. ‘It can’t be more than that. I live here. You go home in a week.’

‘That’s right.’

‘And what will you miss the most from your stay in Portugal?’

‘The coffee.’ I grin and Dylan rolls his eyes at me. ‘And the sun, and the laidback lifestyle, and the people I’ve met.’ I can feel myself blushing.

Dylan nods, saying nothing.

‘I mean, I’m looking forward to seeing Gemma; I’ve really missed her.’

‘But?’

'But I'd be lying if I said I was looking forward to slotting back into my mundane life.'

Dylan shrugs. 'So don't.'

'Don't what?' I ask.

'Don't go back to England. Stay here instead.'

I laugh. 'And what does that look like?'

'It looks like, you stay here. I…I love you.' Dylan says, staring at me intently.

I stop chuckling and look straight at him. 'Oh, you're not joking.'

Dylan shakes his head. 'I'm not joking.'

'You're serious?'

'That's kind of what "I'm not joking" means.'

'So, what? I just wouldn't go home? I would stay here and start a new life? That's crazy.'

'It's not so crazy.'

I take a gulp from my wine glass and Dylan does the same.

'I can't just stay here. I have to go back.'

'Because it's the sensible thing to do and that's who you are, or at least who you are in England.'

I bite my lip. 'Because it's the right thing to do. That's where I live – that's where my job and my friends and family are.'

'And your ex-boyfriend?'

I glare at Dylan, then pick up my glass and drink the remaining wine. 'I'm not doing this,' I say, more sternly than I'd intended. 'I came here to apologise. I said I was sorry, and I meant it.' I push the chair back and stand up.

'Kiera, don't go,' Dylan says, looking up at me. 'Sit down, and let's eat.'

'You know what? I don't think I will, thank you.'

As I turn and walk away, I wipe a tear from my eye. I hear Dylan calling my name, but I don't look back. I can't. My heart won't let me.

By the time I make it back to my apartment my vision is blurred from gathering tears threatening a downpour. I walk through the apartment, making my way to the bedroom, only pausing to remove my wedges before I face-plant onto the bed and sob into the quilt. It's at this point that I finally acknowledge Dylan's words. He said that he loves you.

Chapter Thirteen

I wake with a banging headache. Rubbing my temples does nothing to improve the situation. I slide out of bed and remove last night's dress and underwear, then pull on my dressing gown and head to the kitchen to make a coffee, or three. I squint as the bright sunlight shines through the open blinds and curtains as I plod into the kitchen, feeling weirdly like I'm hungover despite only having had the one glass of wine with Dylan.

One glass of wine.

No dinner.

An argument instead.

Not really what I had expected.

And why did you do that, Kiera? Why did you walk away?

The coffee machine beeps, signalling that my drink is ready. I collect the cup and walk out onto the balcony, leaving the question hanging.

I pull on my sunglasses and drink my coffee quickly before heading back inside for a refill. As I walk into the bathroom for a shower ten minutes later, I catch a glimpse of my reflection in the mirror. A puffy face, bags under my eyes, and last night's mascara smeared down each cheek. I look ridiculous. I feel ridiculous, and embarrassed, and in inner turmoil.

Did Dylan actually say he loves me and asked me to stay in Portugal last night? I mean, that's just crazy, and unthinkable, and so far removed from anything that I could do.

But then you got up and left him.

I had no choice. That was the right thing to do. To end things there, before they could get any more complicated. He said that he loves me.

'So, are you not going to see him again before you leave?' I ask my reflection in the mirror.

I think that's for the best.

After my shower, I head back out onto the balcony. I scroll aimlessly through the long list of texts on my phone between Jacob and me, many of them mundane, some of them more affectionate, but each ending with two kisses. It's amazing how many conversations two people can have over a four-year period. When you put them all together, what does the picture show?

Gemma would kill me if she knew that I kept all of his texts. And why did I? Sentimental value, though I didn't expect to ever see him again – well, not intentionally anyway. There's always that dread of bumping into the ex when you're not looking your best, when you've left the house that one time on a Sunday morning with no makeup on and without brushing your hair to pop to the shop for an emergency packet of coffee beans.

I sip my coffee, but it's already cooled too much and instantly I grimace. I didn't realise how long I had been taking a trip down memory lane. Is that all it is, a trip down memory lane, or is there a path going forward in the future for me and Jacob? Do I really want to go down that road again? I mean, it's safe and comfortable, and when we were good, we were really good together. As I look back now, I can't really remember at what point things went wrong, or why. Maybe that's the problem right there. There were no fireworks, not like with Dylan.

Dylan. Huh. He's definitely something else, and nothing like I've experienced before. His charm, his confidence, his excitement at showing me all the things that he loves here, the way he cocks his head on one side when he's questioning me, his appreciation for good coffee and wine, his love for Portuguese food…I realise that the list could go on, but it isn't real. We're just caught up in a bubble that will burst the minute I get on the plane back to the UK. And we both know that I'm getting on that plane. I mean, I can't stay here, no matter what kind of picture Dylan paints for me. It's absurd.

I can just see how that conversation would go.

'So, Gemma, funny story, I'm not coming home…No, I don't have a job…No, I don't have anywhere to live…No, I don't speak Portuguese.'

I shake my head and get up from the chair on the balcony and take my now-completely-cold coffee through to the kitchen. I pour it down the sink and go about making a fresh one. As the coffee machine comes to life, I stare out of the kitchen window at the bright-blue sky. This view is definitely preferable to that of a dull January day in England, but I'm guessing that they have winter here too. Every day isn't like a summer holiday. People work here, they have bills here, they do mundane things like the food shop and hoovering. That is the reality. That's real life, no matter which country you're in.

No, the sensible thing is to go home as planned, meet up with Jacob, see where it takes us. And maybe it takes us back to where we were, and that could be a good thing. Yes, that's the sensible thing to do.

I cannot allow myself to see Dylan again, to make love to Dylan again, to fall in love with Dylan.

I spend my last five days lolling at the beach, lolling at the poolside, lolling on my sofa with takeaway food, so that I can avoid bumping into Dylan. But that seems unlikely. I've had no texts from him, no calls, nothing. But what did I expect? I got up and walked away from him.

On my last day, I decide to have breakfast at Claudette and Santi's place. I pull on a flowing maxi dress and flipflops, and head out into the morning heat. As I arrive at the restaurant, I can see Claudette clearing tables, and she waves me over.

'It is good to see you, Kiera,' she says, pulling me into an embrace. I hug her back. I'm genuinely going to miss her and Santi. 'Is it your last day?'

'Yes, I fly back tomorrow afternoon, so I thought, what better place to spend my last morning?' I smile.

'Have you seen Dylan?'

I bite my lip. 'No, and I don't expect to.'

'Kiera, I know it is really not my business, but you cannot leave it this way. You must say a proper goodbye to him, yes?'

I shake my head. 'I don't think he's that bothered about seeing me,' I say.

'Rubbish.' Claudette waves her hand dismissively. 'He asked you to stay, yes?'

I raise my eyebrows.

She shrugs. 'Dylan, he talks, you know.'

'So I see.'

Claudette shakes her head. 'I mean no disrespect, Kiera. I have just never seen Dylan like this with anyone. In fact, I have not seen him serious with anyone in the time that I have known him.'

‘Yes, well, that’s, um…’ This is not the conversation I was expecting. ‘Look, I just wanted to say thank you to you and Santi for making me feel so welcome.’

‘Of course, Kiera. It has been lovely to meet you.’

‘And for your shopping guidance.’

Claudette smiles broadly. ‘But of course.’

‘Hey, Kiera.’ Santi strides out of the bar and grabs me in a bear hug. ‘It is your last day?’

‘Unfortunately, yes,’ I say. ‘I fly home tomorrow.’

‘Oh, well, I hope you will make it back here soon.’

‘Definitely,’ I agree.

‘What can I get you to eat?’ Claudette asks.

I think for a moment. ‘You know what, I think today requires pancakes, please, and a very large coffee.’

Santi smiles. ‘Coming right up, Kiera. Take a seat.’

I sit at a table in the corner of their outside seating area and just enjoy the warm sun on my face.

Claudette brings out a coffee and places it in front of me. ‘Free refills for you today.’ She smiles.

‘That’s very kind of you, Claudette. But you might regret that,’ I say.

My phone buzzes and I take a slurp of my coffee before pulling my phone from my handbag. My heart constricts as I see a text from Dylan flashing on the screen. I want to look at it, I really do, but I'm afraid. It's been five days without contact. This is either a peace offering or…I don't want to think about *or*.

I place my phone face down on the table and sip my coffee. Claudette brings a plate of food over to my table.

'Pancakes for your last breakfast with us,' she says, placing the plate down in front of me. 'What is wrong?'

'Nothing,' I say.

She raises her eyebrows.

'Maybe nothing.' I turn the phone over and she looks at the screen.

'What is the message from Dylan?'

'I don't know.'

Claudette sits down. 'You haven't looked at it yet?'

I take a bite of a pancake. 'No.'

'Why not?'

I pause, mid-chew. 'Because I'm afraid of what it might say.'

'Shall I look for you?' she offers.

I put more pancake in my mouth and nod, sliding the phone towards her. Claudette picks it up and looks at the screen. I wait impatiently.

'He says he doesn't want to leave things like this.' Claudette looks at me. 'He wants you to have dinner together one last time.'

I nearly choke on my pancake.

'Do you want that too?' she asks, looking at me expectantly.

I pick up my coffee and take a gulp. 'I guess I'm open to that,' I say.

'Do you want to reply?'

I lean over and take the phone back from Claudette, then read his text before replying:

I would like to clear the air between us, and see you one last time. Italian at eight?

I toss the phone to the end of the table and continue with my breakfast. After a second coffee, I hug Claudette and Santi goodbye, promising to return as soon as I can, then I head back to my apartment to pack. My phone has remained silent throughout, and I'm not sure what to make of that.

I have packed literally everything, other than the essentials that I'll need tomorrow morning before I head to the airport. I'm feeling a mixture of emotions at the realisation that this is my last night here, my last night to see Dylan. He hasn't responded to my earlier text. I shower and dress for dinner regardless, and then at the eleventh hour, my phone beeps.

See you at Santi's at eight

I breathe a sigh of relief at the same time as feeling completely conflicted.

Chapter Fourteen

'I couldn't let you leave without seeing you one last time,' Dylan says, taking a sip of red wine.

I arrived at the restaurant first for a change, and I had a gin and tonic to settle my nerves before Dylan arrived.

'I wasn't sure that you would show,' he says, his gaze fixed on me.

'I wasn't sure that I would either,' I say, taking a sip of my own wine.

'So, what happened the last time we met?' Dylan challenges.

I take a deep breath before saying, 'I think, in my confused mind, I thought it would be better to break up with you then rather than now. I didn't want to fall any deeper.'

'I've missed you over the last few days.' Dylan doesn't take his eyes off me. 'Have you thought about what I said?'

'About staying in Portugal?'

'Yes.'

I shake my head. 'I can't.'

'There's no changing your mind?'

I swallow noisily, 'No, no changing my mind. I came here for a few weeks out of my normal life, and I've loved every second of it, believe me, but now it's time to go home, to go back to reality.'

Dylan reaches his hand across the table, and his fingers brush mine before he wraps them around my hand. My heart constricts. How can I feel so close to somebody I've only just met? I spent two years living with Jacob every day and never felt anything close to the all-consuming, ridiculously inappropriate whatever-it-is that I currently find myself in.

'Can I come to the airport with you tomorrow?' Dylan asks.

'No.'

'No?'

'I can't say goodbye to you like that.'

Dylan looks down, releasing my hand before stuffing his hands under the table. 'So what happens now?'

I breathe in deeply, then exhale. 'We have dinner and enjoy a lovely evening one last time.'

'And at the end of the night?'

'At the end of the night, we say goodnight.'

'Just like that?'

'Just like that.'

He nods sternly, then smiles warmly. 'Then we'd better make the most of tonight. Are you ready for dinner?'

'Ready.' I pick up the menu and study it seriously, even though I know every item listed on here.

We eat food, make small talk, and completely ignore the huge elephant in the room, until we walk back to my apartment for the last time.

We stand in the entrance to the building, the tension between us palpable. The lift pings, announcing its arrival, and with it the realisation that the end is nigh.

'So you don't want me to come up?'

'No.'

'We're saying our goodbyes here in the hallway?'

I glance around. It's pitiful, standing in the cold entrance to the building.

'That's right.'

The lift pings again, apparently frustrated that we've summoned it and then ignored it.

I step into the lift. Dylan steps in after me. He swivels me around to face him. We're only inches apart, our eyes locked. I can feel the heat between us. My entire body is tingling, and then Dylan's lips are on mine, kissing me with an urgency that just fans the flames of desire inside me. We fall out of the lift as it arrives on the third floor and barely make it through the door to my apartment before we're pulling at each other's clothes. It's fast, and frantic, and without doubt the hottest sex I've ever had.

We lie together in the bed, my head resting on his heaving chest as we both catch our breath.

'Now that's more like the kind of goodbye that I was thinking.' Dylan sighs.

'Hmm. I feel like I've been coerced.'

'Coerced?' He chuckles. 'You didn't need any encouragement.'

'Maybe not.' I grin.

Dylan wraps his arm around me, and I snuggle into him.

'I can't do another goodbye.' I wipe a stray tear from my eye before it can make its escape down my cheek. 'Can you do me a favour and wait until I fall asleep before you leave?'

I hear his voice catch in his throat before he says, 'I understand.'

The early-morning sun streaks through the crack in the curtains and I roll over. The other side of the bed is empty, cold and empty. My heart sinks at the realisation that this is it. I will never see Dylan again. I pick up the pillow next to me and inhale deeply. The scent of Dylan's aftershave fills my lungs and then the tears come. I've known this moment was coming, but I had no idea that I would feel so heartbroken.

I make a coffee and sit out on the balcony as the warm morning breeze blows against my cheeks. Well, Portugal, I came here wanting adventure, and boy did you give me one. One that I didn't expect, and one that I wasn't prepared for. But it will be one that I'll never forget.

I pull up in the hire-car car park and manoeuvre the car into the first available space. As I climb out of the air-conditioned vehicle, the wall of heat hits me full in the face and I feel perspiration forming immediately on my forehead, just like when I first arrived. I reach up and wipe my face with the back of my hand before pulling my handbag over my head and lifting my suitcase out of the boot of the car. It weighs considerably less than when I arrived, but maybe that's because I've replaced the toiletries that I've used with new clothes and handbags, which are considerable lighter.

Having dropped the car keys into the 'Returns' box at the car rental office, I walk slowly along the concrete path towards the departure terminal. Inside, the airport is warm, and busy. I can hear numerous languages being spoken over the tannoy as people hustle and bustle, sun-kissed and tired, in anticipation of the long journey home ahead. I take my place in the queue for the check-in for my flight and shuffle along at a snail's pace as the airline staff check in everybody's luggage.

Chapter Fifteen

The wait at the airport seems to last forever. I stare out at the aeroplanes lined up. Baggage handlers are milling around, and I watch the bags being loaded. I sigh heavily. The wait at the airport to fly out was very different. The feeling of anticipation at my trip had made me giddy as I picked up toiletries and perfume in the duty-free shopping. Was that really just a few weeks ago?

Now, my heart feels heavy as I wait for my flight home. I was expecting a few carefree weeks in the sun. I was not expecting to meet someone who would have such an effect on me. Dylan is handsome and kind, with a great sense of humour. He's experienced things in his life that no-one should. I can understand his desire to live the life he lives in Portugal, and why he doesn't want to come back to the UK, but I can't do that. I can't just uproot and move to another country – a country where I don't speak the language, for a start. Whatever my feelings for Dylan, it's just not possible. I live in England, not Portugal. This was a four-week sabbatical from my normal life and that's how I have to leave things.

I wipe a tear from my cheek, pull my phone out of my pocket and stare at the screen for the hundredth time since I left the apartment. Nothing. No texts, no missed calls.

Come on, Kiera, what are you expecting? Some last-minute attempt from him to get you to stay? Dylan told you he loved you and he asked you to stay in Portugal. You said no. That's the end. He's not going to come running after you like some white knight on a horse. This isn't the movies; this is real life. And you made a choice too, a promise to Jacob to at least hear him out. To consider getting back together with him, with an open mind.

I hear my flight called over the tannoy, but my feet feel like lead. I force myself to turn around and walk to the boarding gate and join the back of the queue of holidaymakers, tanned and tired and all heading home. Home, that's a funny thing. Home to me isn't a place as such. Home is Gemma and Tom and their kids. Home is my mum and dad on a Sunday having a roast dinner.

It's not until I board the plane and sit down that I realise how much I've missed home. I can't wait to see Gemma and give her a hug. The new baby will be arriving shortly too. Home was once Jacob, but maybe not anymore. Can I go backwards, no matter how convinced he might be that we made a mistake? I don't know. But I can't go forward with Dylan either, so I guess I'll just stand still for the moment, alone.

As the plane taxis down the runway, I try to put all thoughts of Dylan and Portugal from my mind. No good will come of wallowing in misery for the entire flight home. Once take-off is complete and the seatbelt signs have gone off, I put in my headphones and watch out the window as the glorious golden coastline disappears from sight.

The steward appears at my side. 'Can I get you anything to eat or drink?'

'A gin and tonic, please,' I say. 'Make it a large one.'

The flight home somehow seems so much quicker than the flight out. Maybe it's perception, maybe it's mind games. This is the short, sharp snap back to reality. But what is reality? A job I've had since I was seventeen? Going back to a relationship that's comfortable and predictable? Is this what life is? What if this isn't what life is about? What if it's about taking chances, doing something different, stepping outside your comfort zone? Can that be done? Is that just the stuff of dreams, of fantasies, of the lyrics to some stupid pop song on the radio? Of a handsome man promising a fairy tale? Do fairy tales even exist?

The voice of my own Prince Charming echoes in my ears: *'Don't you want to find out?'*

I jerk sideways as the plane hits the tarmac and the jolt of reality sears through me. I'm back in the UK, and my sabbatical is well and truly over.

We pile off the plane like ants following the line to the terminal building. Once inside, the government officer scowls at my passport, probably wondering what possessed me to have a perm in 2015. Believe me, Mr Immigration Officer, you're not the only one.

I collect my suitcase from the carousel of doom and head out to the arrivals area, where I know Gemma will be waiting for me. I plaster a smile on my face. It's not a total lie; I'm so looking forward to seeing Gemma, and Marnie, and Tom, and I'm excited at the very imminent arrival of my second godchild. But oh my God, my heart aches for the stupid holiday romance that I left behind in Portugal.

Was it a holiday romance, or something more? I guess I'll never know. It was a short escapism from my real life. Although what I was actually trying to escape from is unclear. Was it the mundane, everyday life of nine to five with no-one to come home to, no-one to stop that feeling of emptiness when I turned out the light at night? Was I trying to escape from my failed relationship with Jacob? Was it the fact that my best friend is married with a beautiful daughter and another baby on the way while I have no significant other, and no immediate maternal instinct?

The minute I step into the arrivals area I hear the undeniable screech of Gemma. 'Kiera!'

Within seconds I'm rugby-tackled by Gemma in a huge bear hug. Despite my defiant stance, a tear slips from my eye and slides painfully down my cheek, and I suck in my breath to prevent a complete meltdown.

'I've missed you so much.' Gemma clings on to me with force and I hug her back like my life depends on it.

'I've missed you so much too, like you wouldn't believe.'

My grip tightens and I can hear the thud of my own heartbeat as I squash myself into Gemma's embrace. I have missed her, unbelievably so. But something has changed in the time since I left. A tilt on the scales, in the equilibrium of our friendship. Somehow the solace I used to take for granted in my comfortable life feels like it has been blended in a Nutribullet. I don't even recognise how I feel.

'It's so good to see you.' Gemma pulls away from our embrace.

I smile. 'It's so good to see you too.'

'I missed you, Aunty Kiera.' Marnie slams into me, nearly knocking me off my feet as she flings her arms around me, and I gulp as further tears escape.

'Hey, are you okay?' Gemma squeezes my arm.

I take a deep breath. 'I'm absolutely fine. It's so good to see you all.' I swallow down the emotion that's come from nowhere and is threatening to overwhelm me.

'Welcome home.' Tom takes hold of my suitcase.

'It just hasn't been the same without you,' Gemma says.

I nod, taking deep breaths. Why I'm so emotional is beyond me.

We walk in silence to the car; the only sound is my gulp of emotion as Marnie takes hold of my hand and squeezes it. My heart skips a beat.

Once in the car, Marnie in the front seat and Gemma and me in the back, Gemma turns to me.

'So, how was it, your jolly away from reality?'

I exhale. Was it four weeks away from reality, or four weeks of reality?

'It was great.'

Gemma pulls a face, biting her lip before sitting back. 'Really?'

'Really.' I nod.

Gemma glances over at Tom, then back at me. 'Liar,' she proclaims.

I shake my head. 'No, I had a great time, but I'm glad to be back.'

'No romance after all then?'

Holding back the tears that are threatening to show me up, I say 'Nothing worth talking about.'

Thankfully, Gemma turns and faces out of the window as Tom pulls out into the line of traffic and my broken heart sinks.

The ride home is quiet, and that isn't lost on me; even Marnie seems unsure of what to say. Her usual line of frantic questions is nowhere. As we turn onto my street, Gemma takes hold of my hand.

'I'm so glad to have you back. This baby needs you here.'

'Of course,' I say as we pull up outside my house, which is exactly as I left it. I don't know why I expected it to look any different; maybe it's because I feel like a different person to the one who left only a short time ago. Am I a different person? Can people change that quickly? I don't know.

'I'll grab your case,' Tom says, climbing out of the car. Before going to the boot, he helps Gemma, and her considerable girth, squeeze out of the car too.

I unclip my seatbelt and smile at Marnie, still strapped into her car seat.

'I'm glad you're home,' she says, handing me a sticky sweet that she appears to have been holding in her curled-up hand for the duration of the journey.

I take the sweet with no intention of putting it in my mouth. I have no idea where Marnie has had it.

'Come here,' I say, releasing her from the car seat and wrapping my arms around her. She snuggles into me, and I inhale the smell of sweet strawberry shampoo.

Gemma opens the car door. 'Come on, Marnie, put Kiera down. She must be tired from her journey and in desperate need of a cup of tea.'

I kiss the top of Marnie's head and release her. Gemma isn't wrong: I am tired, and in need of a cuppa. I slide out of the car and take my suitcase from Tom.

'Do you want us to come in?' Gemma asks.

'No,' I say, 'You've done enough, thank you. I think I'm going to collapse on the sofa and catch up on some TV.'

'Good idea. I put milk in your fridge, so you can have a drink. Oh, and also some left-over lasagne – it just needs heating up.'

I smile. 'You're amazing. What would I do without you?'

'I'll call you tomorrow. We can do brunch or something.'

'Definitely.'

I watch as they all climb back in the car and I wave frantically as Tom pulls away. I watch until the car turns right at the end of the street and disappears out of sight.

Opening the front door, I step inside, hoisting my suitcase over the threshold, then close the door behind me. Silence surrounds me and I gaze around. It feels alien. The house still has my décor and furnishings, but it looks different, feels different, from when I left, like something is missing. Maybe it is. Maybe something is missing from me. Maybe I left a part of me in Portugal, a part of me that I'll never get back.

I need to snap out of this. I need to start getting back to normal. It was only four weeks. Nothing here has really changed; it just feels like it has. Everything in my life is exactly the same, just a little further down the line.

Four weeks seems like a short period of time, but is it, actually? Dylan's words from when we were on the boat in my first week in Portugal play back through my mind. He told me how his life had changed in an instant. It only takes a minute for your life to change. It only takes a minute to fall in love.

Sod the cup of tea; I need something stronger. Walking through to the kitchen, I pray that I didn't drink all the Sauvignon Blanc before I left. I'm relieved to find that I didn't, and a bottle is nestled, fully chilled, on the wine shelf in the fridge. I take out the bottle and pour myself a large glass, ignoring the nagging voice in my head reminding me that it's only three thirty in the afternoon. If I was still in Portugal, sitting in the sun, I wouldn't bat an eyelash at consuming alcohol in the middle of the afternoon. I'll go back to being sensible from Monday when I go back to work, but until then I think I'll continue my sabbatical lifestyle.

I take a gulp of wine. The crisp, fruity liquid is both refreshing and satisfying. I pull my phone out of my handbag and glance at the screen. No text from Dylan. I toss the phone onto the kitchen worktop. What was I expecting? That I would land in the UK and we would remain text friends? No, I made my choice. This is it. Go for brunch with

Gemma tomorrow. Meet Jacob for a trip down memory lane.

I take another gulp from my glass. Is this it? Is this really what I'm going to do with the rest of my life?

I inhale deeply, pick up my mobile phone, exhale loudly, then down the remaining wine. I count to three in my head before pressing the fourth speed-dial in my contacts. The call is answered after two rings.

'Pete's Taxis,' a gruff voice growls down the phone, customer service at its finest.

'Hi, yes, I need a taxi, please.'

'When for?'

'Now, as soon as you can.'

'Where from?'

'Dunham Road, number twenty-one.'

'And where to?'

'To the airport, please.'

Epilogue

My phone beeps and a text from Gemma flashes on the screen. I click into it and scroll through the pictures that appear of Gemma, Tom, and Marnie, and of course Elliott, who isn't so small anymore. I can't believe that he's ten months old. Marnie has her arm wrapped around him in a protective big sister manner that's perhaps bordering on strangulation, but Elliott doesn't seem to mind. He grins a gummy smile. They look so happy, and a ping of sadness washes over me that I'm not there with them.

'Hey.' Dylan drapes his arm over me from behind and kisses my cheek. 'How was your day at work?'

'Good, thanks.' I look up to meet his gaze.

'Photos from Gemma?'

'Yeah. Elliott is getting so big.'

'It won't be long until they visit next month.'

'I know; I can't wait to see them all.'

He sits down in the chair next to me on the balcony. The warm orange sun is starting to set. 'I was thinking,' he says, 'it's a year today since we met.'

I try hard to hide my smile at the fact he has remembered. 'Is it?' I say nonchalantly.

Dylan raises his eyebrows. 'I know that you know it is.'

I smile. 'So what were you thinking?'

'Well…' He leans forward. 'I thought we should do something that we did when we first met.'

'I'm not going skinny-dipping,' I say sternly. 'That was a one-time thing.'

Dylan chuckles. 'What I had in mind was more like dinner at the Italian, maybe a little too much red wine, followed by lying on the sand staring up at the stars.'

'That sounds perfect.' I lean in and kiss him gently on the lips.

'Then we can make love into the early hours,' he whispers in my ear.

After a fabulous meal at the Italian, and, as Dylan suggested, a little too much red wine, we lie on the beach staring up at the starry sky.

I sigh contentedly. ‘I never get tired of looking at this view.’

‘Me neither.’ Dylan rolls over onto his side so he’s facing me. ‘So, no regrets about your life in Portugal?’

‘Our life,’ I correct him, rolling to face him.

‘Of course.’ He grins. ‘Although it didn’t take you long to make it back here. What was it? A three-hour turnaround from landing in the UK to getting back on a plane? I guess you missed me that much.’

‘Not that much.’ I shrug. ‘It was at least four hours.’

Dylan laughs, and I can’t help but laugh too. It *was* ridiculous that I returned to Portugal less than twelve hours after leaving. I actually did miss him that much, but I'm not going to massage his ego by telling him that.

'Seriously, though.' And he actually does look serious now. 'No regrets about moving to Portugal? I know you miss your family; Gemma, Marnie.' He rolls sand between his fingertips.

I reach over and place my hand over his. 'Absolutely no regrets. I love my life here; and most of the time I love you.' I smile.

Dylan rolls his eyes at me. 'I love you too.'

'And my friends and family are only a couple of hours' flight away.'

'Of course.'

'Do you remember when we were just friends with benefits?' I say.

Dylan laughs softly. ‘You made me work for those benefits.’

‘Maybe I should make you work for those benefits more often.’

Dylan shakes his head. ‘You want to play hard to get?’

I roll over and lie back looking up at the stars.

‘I told you from the beginning, that’s not my style,’ Dylan says, leaning in to kiss me.

The touch of his lips on mine still makes me tingle, even after a year. I still can’t quite believe that I live in Portugal and have a whole different life to when I set off on what I thought would be a one-month sabbatical, experiencing a new country for a short time.

I think back to Claudette's words that first week that I spent here: "It only takes a minute to fall in love." She was right, kind of. I think the connection I had with Dylan was there from the instant that I, literally, bumped into him, even if I didn't realise it then.

'Come on,' Dylan says, brushing my lips gently with his thumb, causing my insides to flip excitedly. 'We did dinner, we had wine, we've looked up at the stars, now let's make love into the early hours.'

He pulls me to my feet and takes my hand, and as we stroll back across the sand, I have to pinch myself. It still seems surreal that I'm here, with Dylan, loving my life in Portugal. I snuggle closer into him, feeling the warmth of his body against mine. Was it fate that day that we bumped into each other on the square, or just a chance meeting? I don't know, but either way, it just shows that your life can change in a minute, sometimes in the most amazing way, and I'm very thankful that I'm living proof of that.

The End

Thank you for taking the time to read my book; I hope you enjoyed it. If you did, I'd really appreciate it if you could take a moment to leave me a review on your favourite retailers' website.

Thanks!

Sasha x

Printed in Great Britain
by Amazon

23353333R00185